WITHDRAWN

①

LONGHORN TRAIL

Center Po
Large Pr

**This Large Print Book carries the
Seal of Approval of N.A.V.H.**

LONGHORN TRAIL
A Western Duo

LAURAN PAINE

CENTER POINT PUBLISHING
THORNDIKE, MAINE

A Circle Ⓥ Western published by
Center Point Large Print in co-operation with
Golden West Literary Agency.
First Edition December 2009.

Copyright © 2009 by Mona Paine.

"The Killing at Pipestone" first appeared in
Real Western Stories (2/56).
Copyright © 1956 by Columbia Publications, Inc.
Copyright © renewed 1984 by Lauran Paine.
Copyright © 2009 by Mona Paine for restored material.

The text of this Large Print edition is unabridged.
Printed in the United States of America.
Set in 16-point Times New Roman type.

ISBN: 978-1-60285-609-7

Library of Congress Cataloging-in-Publication Data

Paine, Lauran.
  Longhorn trail : a western duo / Lauran Paine. -- 1st ed.
    p. cm.
  ISBN 978-1-60285-609-7 (library binding : alk. paper)
  1. Large type books. I. Paine, Lauran. Killing at Pipestone. II. Title.

PS3566.A34L66 2009
813'.54--dc22

2009033251

TABLE OF CONTENTS

The Killing at Pipestone

I

The girl asked: "Why do they call it Pipestone, mister?"

Jack looked down at her with a sympathetic little grin. "There's a red stone quarry on the ranch where the Indians used to dig up the rock an' make pipes out of it. Calumets they're called. The pipes, I mean." He rolled a cigarette thoughtfully. "The Cole family's owned this ranch for four generations. I'm the last of them. It's always been called the Pipestone."

"Oh." She was a small wisp of a girl with a piquant, small oval of a face. Her eyes were large, expressive, and very blue and her figure couldn't be improved on. It was sturdy and shapely, with strong, hard hips and a large bosom.

Jack looked at her and shook his head wryly. "You were darned lucky, Miss . . . ?"

"Julie Krohn."

"Awfully lucky, Miss Julie, that that darned horse didn't kill you, runnin' off like that and tryin' to jump the Big Hole Cañon with you."

Her face blanched at the recollection. "Yes. I don't know what made him do that."

"Where d' ya live, Miss Julie?"

Her eyes swept up his husky figure and stopped at his soft brown eyes. He read the fright and stubbornness in them and remembered her little valise

then, with its feminine apparel scattered over the brush. It hit him all of a sudden. She had a secret and wasn't going to tell him.

He shrugged; it wasn't really important, anyway. The important thing was that he'd saved her by happening along and roping her before she went to the bottom of the cañon with the runaway horse, and now she was sitting on the couch in his ranch house. He smiled reassuringly at her. It was a good smile with a lot of easy charm in it.

"Forget I asked, Miss Julie. I'll get us some supper."

She jumped up eagerly, her eyes adoring every inch of him. "I'll help. I'm really a good cook." He looked at her standing up and admired the stocky wholesome strength of her even more. Then his eyes dropped irresistibly to the torn V of her blouse and the satin swelling of her breasts where they showed above it. She flushed frantically and caught the two halves in one hand. "Do you have a pin?"

"In the kitchen."

They went into the room; he handed her a pin and started building a fire in the box of the stove. She mended the dress as best she could—which wasn't too well—then smilingly hustled in to help.

It wasn't long before Jack Cole felt acutely aware of his own awkwardness. Little Julie had no waste motion. She fried the steaks, slashed up a tossed salad, and fried potatoes all at once. Jack set

the table with his customary laborious diligence and saw her grinning slyly at his efforts. He smiled ruefully and thought to himself that, before the month was out, Beth would have charge of things on the Pipestone and everything would be different. He was lost in the thoughts of Beth Morgan and her dark, heady beauty. He thrilled again to each kiss they had exchanged, and their love. He wasn't conscious of his silent moodiness until Julie looked up at him anxiously, her expressive eyes showing a hint of pathos.

"Did I do something wrong? Isn't your steak done, Jack?"

He felt guilty when he looked at the piquant little face and smiled at her affectionately. "Miss Julie, I was ten miles away. I was over at Railhead, dreaming."

"Oh." She had a way of saying it, then dropping her head, that made every man she had ever known want to put an arm around her. It was a sort of helpless, little-girl gesture and she did it unconsciously. He watched her eat like a young wolf and rolled a cigarette with a wry smile.

"Miss Julie, I don't care what your past has been, or where you came from, but one thing I *would* like to know, just for the heck of it. When did you eat last?"

"Yesterday morning, Jack." She threw him a rapturous smile. "And this is awfully good beef. Pipestone?"

11

He nodded his head with a hint of pride.

She winked and rolled her head ecstatically with a mischievous twinkle in her eyes. "It's heavenly."

"You're just hungry."

The wind started to blow hard about 8:00 p.m. They were sitting in front of the fire and listening to it when Jack got drowsy. He yawned and smiled across the room at her. "Excuse me a minute, Miss Julie." He got up, went into his room, got a pair of pajamas from the dresser, and gave them to her, pointing to a side door off the living room. "There's a spare bedroom there, Miss Julie. Good bed, too." He smiled down at her. "G' night."

"Jack?"

He was half across the room, then he turned. "Yes?"

"Thanks." Her eyes were grateful, like the eyes of a stray dog that's been rescued out of a storm and fed. He knew what she meant, too. Thanks for not asking a lot of questions. He felt a surge of pity for her.

"You're plumb welcome, Miss Julie. G' night."

"Good night, Jack."

II

He made it to Railhead by 10:00 the next morning and tied the buggy outside of Calvenger's Emporium, went in, gave old Samuel the list of groceries, and told him where the buggy was, then he headed uptown toward the bank. Banker Claude Miller was just entering the building when Jack walked up. He smiled affably and held the door open for him. The Cole family account had been the sole support of the Railhead Stockman's Banking Company in more than one financial panic.

"Come on into my office, Jack. We'll visit for a spell. There's not likely to be much business for a while anyway."

Jack entered the office with a smile and dropped into one of the cane-backed chairs against the wall. He watched Claude Miller spread his ample girth out in his swivel chair. "What time does Dan get here, Claude?"

The banker's eyes clouded a trifle and the smile slid off his face. "Dan Morgan? Oh, he'll be along directly." He studied Jack for a silent second, then leaned forward on his desk. "I'm glad you brought old Dan up, Jack. He's been on my mind quite a bit lately." Miller shook his head ruefully. "Somethin' wrong with Dan, Jack." He tapped his fingers restlessly on the desk top. "You're engaged to Beth, aren't you?"

Jack nodded soberly. He had wondered a little about Beth's father, too, of late. The way he was always on edge and jumpy and his secret trips into the back country.

"Well, to tell the truth, Jack, I'm going to have to dismiss him if he doesn't straighten out." Miller sighed resignedly. "I hate to say it, Jack . . . especially to you, who's on the board of directors of the bank, an' fixin' to marry Dan's daughter, too . . . but the truth is, Jack, I'm gettin' a little leery of him." He frowned and held up a hand when the rancher's brow furrowed. "Oh, it's nothin' I can put my hand on, y' know. It's just that I can't afford to have anyone around the bank that's . . . well, actin' sort o' odd an' shifty like. Y' see my point, Jack?"

"I reckon, Claude." Jack looked thoughtfully out the window at Railhead, with its brave attempt to outgrow the cow town designation the railroads had pinned appropriately on it many years before. This was more serious than he had thought. He looked gravely at Miller. "Don't do anything until I have a talk with Dan, will you? Maybe I can find out his trouble an' get him back on his feet. Hell, Claude, he's been with the bank longer than you or I've been around. He's an old man, now, too. Any disgrace'd just about break him up."

"I know it, Jack." Miller was silent for a moment, frowning down at a note pad on his desk.

"All right, Jack. I'll let it ride until you an' I can thresh it out one way or the other in the next few days." He smiled easily, expansively. "Old Dan's probably at his window by now, Jack, if you want a word with him."

Jack nodded and left the banker's little private cubicle. He saw Dan Morgan shuffling through papers behind his caged-in window and noticed how sunken Beth's father's eyes had become of late. Still wondering at the change in Dan Morgan, he strolled over to his window. "Howdy, Dan."

The teller was startled and jumped violently, then flushed a dark red and forced a ghastly smile. "Give me a start, Jack. Damned if ya didn't. Didn't know you were in town." He spit the explosive little sentences out as if he wanted to cover up his original fright.

Jack frowned slightly. "Listen, Dan. I want you to do me a favor. Drive out to the ranch this evening for supper. Bring Beth, of course. Will you?"

"Sure, son. Sure, we'd be glad to. Thanks. Yes, sir. We'll be out about an hour and a half after the bank closes. Thanks, Jack." His head bobbed up and down like it was on a string. "But, say, hadn't you better go down to the house and tell Beth? I mean, she might have some church doin's planned or something, y' know."

"I reckon so, Dan. I was goin' by, anyway." He grinned fleetingly, almost shyly. "You know I

15

wouldn't leave Railhead without seeing her." He saw Dan's wistful little smile before he turned and walked out of the bank.

It was close to 1:00 p.m. before he started out of Roper's Saloon, where he'd been shanghaied by a bunch of roistering ranchers he'd met after leaving the bank, and jostled in for a few drinks. Jack Cole was a man of many friends in the territory. Finally laughing and shrugging off the razzing, he left the bar and was walking toward the door, his friends teasing him unmercifully, when the doors themselves swung inward and Deputy Buzz Peters was framed in the opening, standing, spraddle-legged, and staring at him menacingly.

The saloon quieted as the watchers sensed Peters's grimness. The deputy's words were like a thunderbolt. They fell on a dumb, awed gathering of cowmen. "Jack Cole, I arrest you fer the murder o' that girl that's livin' with you at your ranch!"

Jack was too dumbfounded to protest or question Peters as he was disarmed of his father's old .44 and led across the hushed roadway to the jail and locked up. Buzz Peters's tight, cold features and bitter eyes spoke volumes, but Jack didn't even speak to him until the numb feeling had worn off, then he banged on the bars until the deputy came sauntering back down the corridor, contempt oozing out of every pore.

"Buzz, tell me about it? Was it Miss Julie? I

mean, was it that short, pretty girl that was out . . . ?"

"You ought to know, Jack." The deputy's cold eyes cut into him. "Nice job you did, hittin' her over the head, an' then hangin' her to a rafter so's it'd look like suicide." He shook his head balefully. "Well, when Clem Miller found her hangin' there, wearin' your pajamas, he come back an' got me an' Doc Hollister. Doc said it was a good try, but it had to be murder because she couldn't very well knock herself out, then hang herself, too." Peters's mouth pulled down into a sour grimace. "I can forgive a man a lot o' things, Jack, but, by God, not a thing like that." He pushed off the wall and turned contemptuously away.

"Hold on a minute, Buzz."

The deputy hesitated and faced half around. "Well?"

"What time did Doc say it happened?"

"Let's quit playin' guessin' games, Jack. You're guilty as hell and we both know it."

"Buzz, I swear I never killed that girl. I've been gone from the ranch since around eight-thirty this mornin'. Been in town ever since, too. I can prove it by Claude Miller, Sam Calvenger, an'. . . ."

"Sure, you're no fool. You'd have proof fairly drippin' off ya. But that girl's still dead, Jack Cole, an' by God I hope you get swung fer it." He walked back two abrupt steps and glared at the prisoner. "An' I hope you're satisfied, too, fer breakin' Beth's heart. Miz Appleby just come by

17

an' said Beth's had a breakdown . . . whatever in hell *that* is. Anyway, I hope you're happy now, livin' with that kid while you're fixin' to marry another girl, then stranglin' her or somethin' because she was goin' to squawk when you told her you was goin' to marry Beth Morgan." He glowered at Jack through the bars. "God! A man never knows another *hombre*, I'm learnin' in this law business. Even old Dan Morgan had to go home from the bank, all broke up an' whimperin'." Peters shook his head slowly from side to side.

"Hold on a minute, Buzz. Who . . . ?"

"Don't Buzz me, Jack Cole."

"Who told you I was living with Julie an' killed her so's she wouldn't raise hell over my marrying Beth? Who's idea was that?"

"Clem Miller told Doc an' me. He says he's seen you moonin' around the ranch with that girl fer a week or more. Lie out of *that*, Mister Cole!" Peters turned abruptly and stalked out of the cell-block, his spurs ringing softly under the impact of his irate footsteps.

Jack slumped on the sagging old bunk nailed against one adobe wall. It was overwhelming. In one short hour, he had been thrown from an eminence of respectability that it had taken four generations of Coles to create in the territory, his friends had apparently melted away, his fiancée was in seclusion, broken up and sick with grief. Worst of all, he could see pathetic little Julie dangling from

18

a rafter in the old ranch house, still wearing his too large pajamas, her tongue hanging blackly from her mouth, and her eyes protruding in abysmal horror. He bent over and covered his face. He was still sitting that way an hour later when three men trouped down the corridor to see him.

"Jack?"

He looked up at Claude Miller's stern, cold face and saw U.S. Marshal Will Olds behind him, his eyes hooded under their perpetual squint, and Dr. Hollister, tall, cadaverous, and solemn with a lot of the human understanding washed forever from his features by the grisly tasks he had performed on the frontier. He stood up mechanically and nodded. The banker looked past his face at the wall, as though the very sight of him was too overpowering for decent men.

"Jack, we've come to hear your side of this murder."

Jack read the condemnation in the banker's eyes. He shrugged dismally. "Claude, you've known me all my life. We've gone hunting together. We punched cows before you went into the bank. Do you think I killed that girl?"

Miller pursed his lips, still avoiding the desperate prisoner's face. "I'm no judge, Jack. All we want is your part of it. Why did you kill her?"

Jack looked at them in horror. They believed it, too. He let the air out of his lungs in a mighty gasp. Actual fear clutched his heart, then. The circum-

stantial evidence was building up too heavily, and suddenly he saw it as they did. He lived alone. Miss Julie was wearing his pajamas, her clothes in the spare bedroom. All of it, the whole sordid mess traced itself out slowly before his mind's eye. His approaching marriage to Beth Morgan. He went back and sank down weakly on the bed.

"I didn't kill her, Claude. I saved her from a runaway yesterday afternoon and brought her home. It was late, Claude. I couldn't make her sleep in the hayloft, could I? She was scared stiff of something."

"What?" It was Marshal Olds. His hooded, unblinking eyes bored into Jack.

"I don't know. She wouldn't talk about it and I didn't insist."

Dr. Hollister's sepulcher voice interrupted scratchily: "If you rescued her yesterday, Cole, how come Clem Miller's seen you with her on the range for the past week or so?"

"That's a damned lie! I never. . . ."

"Jack Cole, my brother's no liar!" Claude Miller was glaring at him. His lips curled downward at their corners. "A filthy, rotten whelp like you callin' Clem a liar." He turned to the others with an eloquent shrug. "I reckon that proves he's guilty as hell, doesn't it? Draggin' decent folk down into the scum with him." The banker cast a withering glance at Jack and started up the aisle toward the deputy's office. Hollister turned abruptly and started away.

Jack watched them go with an awful sinking sensation in his stomach. He grabbed the bars and looked at the marshal. "Will, I don't know what this is all about. I'll swear one thing, though."

"Yeah," Olds said dryly. "You already said it. You didn't kill the girl."

"I didn't, Will. Listen, did you go out to the ranch?"

"No, not yet. I'm goin' as soon as I leave here."

"Then do one thing for me, Will. Look at the girl's clothing. If she'd been at my place for a week, she'd've worn more than one change of clothes, wouldn't she?" He didn't give the marshal a chance to answer. "And if she'd torn her dress, like she did, when that damned horse tried to kill her at Big Hole Cañon, she'd've sewed it up inside of a week or two, wouldn't she?"

"I reckon. Sounds logical, anyway."

"All right then. When you get out there, look at her clothes."

Olds nodded slowly, speculatively. "Fair enough. I'd've done it anyway." He studied Jack for a long moment, then spoke softly. "Something's awful odd here, Cole." He pushed away from the wall.

"What d'ya mean, odd?"

"Don't know yet, but, fer one thing, how come so many men here in Railhead are so hot after you all of a sudden. Both Millers, the doc, an' from

21

what I gather, even your fiancée's dad." He shook his head a little in puzzlement. "Almost too many, Cole, fer such short notice. 'Course, I'll agree it's about the dirtiest crime I ever run across, but still . . . well, I got a feelin' something's awful wrong here."

Jack was hanging to a very weak straw. His desperation was mirrored in his face, too. "Will, won't you come back here when you return from the ranch?"

The marshal looked at him for a long second, then shrugged. "Won't promise, Jack. After all, this is really a local law affair." He started away. "We'll see," he said as he moved toward the deputy's office.

III

Buzz Peters brought a tray with a tin bowl to the cell without unlocking it. Jack's mind had recovered from the awful numbing shock and had been working smoothly since the marshal had left. He looked at the deputy when he shoved the tray under the door with a crooked smile.

"Buzz, answer one question for me, will you?"

"What?" Peters raised his veiled eyes a little and the prisoner was shocked at the rabid hatred that shone out of them.

"What was Clem Miller doing out at my ranch when he found the dead girl?"

"He didn't say. Anyway, it don't make no difference."

"No," Jack said dryly. "I don't suppose it does to you, at that."

It was about an hour later, when the night jailer was on duty and Buzz Peters had gone home, that Will Odds returned. Jack looked up wearily as the marshal stopped outside of his cell.

"Had any visitors since I left, Jack?"

"No, only Buzz. Why?"

Olds built a cigarette and offered Jack the makings. "Well, there seems to be a little steam gettin' up around the saloons to string you up." Olds took back the tobacco sack and held a match for Cole's quirly. "Also, there's eight or ten men who're for you, oddly enough, saying they've known you too long to believe you'd kill a girl like that. But mainly, I was wonderin' if any outsiders had been in to see you. Strangers, I mean."

Jack was smoking in puzzled silence. "What strangers?"

Olds shrugged, looked up the hallway toward the deputy's office, saw the door was closed, and hunkered down close to the bars. There was a sudden excited gleam in his hooded eyes. "Strangers that'd try an' shoot a man down in a jail cell because they figger he might've learned somethin' from a dead girl."

Jack's brows drew together. "Look, Will, I

haven't the faintest damned idea what you're talkin' about. Bring me up to date. Did you look at the clothes like I asked you to?"

Olds nodded, watching his cigarette tip consume brown paper and golden flakes of tobacco. "Yeah, I looked at her clothes." He took a deep drag off the cigarette and faced the prisoner. "Listen, Cole, I'm one man in Railhead who knows you didn't kill that girl. Her name, incidentally, was Julie Krohn."

"Yeah, I know. She told me that much."

"All right. You didn't kill her for two reasons. First, an' maybe least important in Railhead, is that you had no call to. Second, and most important to me as a lawman, is the fact that she's not Julie Krohn. She's Julie Billings, a girl I sent out to get in with Dodge Kennedy, who the government wants fer smugglin'." He arose with a stiff-legged grunt and stepped on the cigarette before he looked back at Cole. "That's what I was afraid of this mornin' when the wire came down the line that a short, well-built girl had been hanged at Railhead. That's why I come up here an' nosed around when it wasn't strictly a federal or territorial matter."

Jack sighed. "Will, I'll do anything I can to help you get her killers. She was about the nicest. . . ."

"Yeah, wasn't she, though?" Olds eyes flared strangely and his jaw muscles rippled along the edge of his face. "I was awful fond of her, Cole." He spat on the floor.

"Tell Peters to let me out of here, then, will you? I've got to see Beth and tell her. . . ."

"Nothin' doin'. You want to help Julie? All right, stay right here an' let the damned muscle heads in Railhead think you're a killer, Jack. It'll be the best thing you could do for her. I'll be free do a little sneakin' around that way. Get it?"

"But Beth? She thinks I'm. . . ."

"I know. That part of it's damned hard, Jack, but it's for the best cause I know of. Don't even tell Peters you've talked to me about this thing. Don't say nothin' to nobody, see? Nothin' at all. Not one word. Play the part like you have been."

Olds stopped talking suddenly and cocked his head a little. A deep, frightening rumble came faintly to them through the adobe walls. Now and then a profane scream would rise hysterically over the deeper sound of shouting, excited men marching. In an instant Jack knew what it was. A lynch mob!

Stunned, the prisoner looked at the U.S. marshal. "It can't be, Will. I know most of those men. I was born an' raised here. They wouldn't do. . . ."

"Don't fool yourself. There's four strangers in Railhead, Jack. I saw 'em myself, an' I know two of 'em. Dodge Kennedy's men. They've been buyin' liquor an' stirrin' up trouble fer two, three hours." He nodded wryly. " 'Sides, a man never knows who his friends are till somethin' like this crops up. The best ones turn out to be the rottenest

of the lot, sometimes. Why, hell, when I went to put up my horse at the livery barn an' old devil white-headed as a cotton boll lit into me with a tongue lashin' I should've killed him for, when I asked what they thought of you."

Jack nodded slowly. "Old Sam Calvenger. Owns the Emporium here. Been like an uncle to me ever since I could walk. He was an old trail drover with my pa."

Olds listened to the mob getting closer. He straightened up with a frown. "Looks like I'll have to get out, after all, dammit. Those Kennedy men are sure spoilin' my plans. I'll go get the keys from the jailer."

He started toward the office door when it suddenly flew open and Buzz Peters, slit-eyed and crouched, faced the marshal. "No, you won't, Marshal. I been listenin' just inside the door. You won't get him out of there, an' furthermore you're goin' to get accidentally killed when the mob gets in here."

The marshal's hard eyes were wide and unblinking. "You, too, Peters? That makes five of you I know here in Railhead." He slouched a little. "All right, if I'm a goner, tell me somethin', just so I won't be wonderin' when I get on the other side. Who's Dodge Kennedy?"

Peters's eyes flamed craftily. "You'd like to know that one, wouldn't you, lawman? Well, you never will."

26

Jack was watching in horrified fascination. He couldn't see Olds's face or he'd have known that the marshal was watching the deputy's mouth for that tiny sucking back every gunman makes a split second before he goes for his guns. Deputy Peters made it and a blur of rocketing, lividly blinding color erupted inside the gloomy cell-block. Two guns exploded almost as one. Olds's second shot followed the falling body down, then he cursed, swung past the dead man, and disappeared inside the office. There was a loud crash, and he was running back down the cell-block with a ring of keys in his hands.

"Get out, Cole." Olds was panting and feverish-eyed. He unlocked the door with nervous fingers and pointed to the dead deputy. "Change clothes with him an' leave him on your bunk. Fast, man, your life depends on it."

Jack thought he'd never finish dressing the warm, loose-jointed corpse. He made a wry face as he pinned the badge on Peters's smelly shirt and dabbed at the sticky blood below the pockets, one on each side. He looked over at the marshal. "Where's the night jailer?"

"Asleep. I broke a chair over his damned head. Hurry up, dammit!"

They darted for the back entrance just as the front door groaned under the impact of a great log in the wild hands of the shrieking lynch mob.

Will peeked out and swore. "Damned place's

surrounded." He swung to Jack. "I'll blow out that lantern in back of us an' you poke your head out the window here an' tell 'em to hurry around in front. Be sure they see Peters's star an' hat. They'll think you're him." He was moving toward the lamp when they heard the front door splinter and give a little under the pounding of the mob's log. Even the palms of Jack Cole's hands were cold and slippery when he called to the guards at the rear door of the jail.

"Around in front, *hombres*, quick. He'll be comin' out as soon as I open his cell. Hurry up, dammit, or you'll miss the fun." Several of the men swore excitedly and started to run. A big, burly man he recognized as Mark Calvenger looked over at him and nodded with a harsh smile. "Thanks," he rumbled, and squinted at Jack's face under the pulled down hat, hesitated, then laughed uproariously and followed the others. Will Olds tore at the grilled door, flung it open, gun in hand, and ran wildly out into the night. Jack was hard behind him when he heard the front door fly off its massive hinges and fly across the deputy's office with a rending crash. The night was wild and alive with savage screams as drunken cowboys ripped the jail to shreds.

Marshal Olds stopped at the far end of Railhead, panting and white-faced. "Never was meant for a runner," he gasped. "Jack, steal a horse offen the racks an' ride for it. I can't go

with you because I want to be seen in town for a while so they won't think I helped you. Hide in your hayloft at the ranch. I'll be out there before dawn. Wait for me." He was gone suddenly, slipping into the shadows of the darkness like he was made of gloom himself.

Jack picked a good, deep-chested, heavily muscled bay horse, untied him in the almost deserted lower end of town, and swung into the saddle. He slapped the dead deputy's six-gun grimly and was wheeling away when he saw a powerfully built shadow disengage itself from the side of a building and come toward him.

"Don't shoot," the man said hastily. "It's me, Mark. Mark Calvenger. I recognized you under Peters's hat, Jack."

He still came on and Cole's hand suddenly rose over the swells of the saddle with a cocked six-gun. They had grown up together, still, as Olds had said, a man never knew who his friends were in a pinch.

Calvenger stopped beside the powerful bay horse and looked up at him sardonically. "Look, Dad an' I know you didn't kill that little girl an' we're all for you, Jack, any way we can be, but"—his eyes traveled over the horse wistfully—"take it easy on him. He's my favorite cutting horse."

Jack eased off the hammer of the gun and grinned wryly. "I didn't know whose critter he was, Mark." He nodded as he reined away. "I'll

turn him loose out on the range. He'll come home, won't he?"

"Oh, sure. I raised him from a colt. He knows where home is all right." The massive, columnar neck swiveled a little and Calvenger's eyes swept back upward. "Jack?"

"Yeah?"

"Before you leave Railhead, go see Beth, boy. She's in pretty bad shape. Ma told us at dinner."

"I'll do it, Mark . . . and thanks."

As Jack reined away, Mark Calvenger listened to the wild shouting that made the night hideous up by the jailhouse. "A double murderer, by God!" he heard someone shouting. "We gotta find him, men! Nobody's safe till he's killed!" Frowning, Mark started up the plank walk toward the surging mass of dark silhouettes careening and howling like imps from hell.

Jack hid the big bay horse in Morgan's dilapidated little barn and crept up to the house. He peeked in, saw that Dan's hat and coat were missing from the great spread of buck's horns by the door, and let himself in the back door. The house was quiet and ghostly with only the weak light of a sickly moon coming in the windows. Carefully he slipped toward Beth's room, listened cautiously, and lifted the latch. Beth was sitting up in bed, her mass of black hair like an ebony halo around her pale face. The startled, large eyes, a deep shade of smoky gray, stared at him in shock.

"Jack!" It came out of her in horror. He put his fingers to his lips and shook his head back and forth to warn for silence, stepped into the room, and closed the door behind him. A tiny reading lantern was on the nightstand next to her bed. He nodded toward it and she reached over and quickly blew it out.

"Darling." He was on the edge of the bed holding her against him. He felt her stiffen a little, fighting against the compelling urge to surrender to this man that she loved so very, very much. He pushed her away and stared down into the anguish in her eyes. "Beth, you know I didn't do it, don't you?"

She was looking into his face with a desperate hunger, searching for something she needed to see there. "You didn't kill her, Jack. Oh, I know you aren't capable of that." He felt the shudder break over her before she spoke again. "But she was living . . . she was wearing your pajamas, Jack. Oh, Jack!" The bitterness ran over and she fell back on the pillow, sobs tearing through her like waves of searing torture.

"Darling, listen to me." He caressed her warm, velvety flesh where the shoulder straps of her nightdress had slipped away. "Please, Beth, I can't stay much longer. There's a lynch mob. . . ."

She came up suddenly, horror glistening through the tears. He caught a fleeting glimpse of her throat, and then she was hugging him hard, the fragrance of her black hair like nectar in his nostrils.

31

"Oh, no! Don't let them. Oh, Jack, run. Leave the country, darling. I'll wait and come to you wherever you are." Her body was quaking in terror. "I don't care if she was living with you. I love you so, Jack."

Her drawn, frightened face came up and his mouth went down gently over her lips. A searing flame of unleashed primeval hunger roared through him. Her full mouth quivered under the pressure, then she was pulling him down to her. He had a wild, crazy desire to stay there on the bed beside her and let them find him there. At least he'd have stolen a moment or two of paradise, then he checked his flaming passions and drew away, shaking his head.

"No, Beth. I don't want it that way. You don't, either. I didn't kill her and she wasn't living with me. I'd only rescued her the afternoon before she was . . . was hanged. She was so little, Beth, and so sort of helpless. Like a little girl. Beth, darling, I wanted you to hear about it from me." He got up and let his hands slip off of her. Suddenly she remembered and pulled the coverlet up where the shoulder straps had slipped.

"Listen, Beth. I have friends and we're tryin' to figure this thing out. There's something awfully big going on. Buzz Peters was in on it, too. The U.S. marshal shot him about a half an hour or so ago. We're riding, honey, but when it's over, I'll be back." He was moving through the darkness when

he spoke again. "Don't tell anyone I was here or what I told you, Beth. You'll be marked for death. Don't even tell your dad. If you want me, darling, see the U. S. marshal . . . *hombre* named Will Olds . . . or Mark Calvenger. Don't trust another living soul, sweetheart, or you'll be in deadly danger. Remember I love you, Beth, more than anything on earth, an' we'll be together as soon as this thing's ironed out."

IV

Jack approached the Pipestone in a great circle that carried him through a lot of cattle bedded down, wearing his iron. He relaxed when he noticed how the cattle leaped up at his approach, and fled. No one was close or his wild range cattle wouldn't be lying down. A mile from the buildings he unbuckled the reins from Mark's bay horse, tied them securely to the saddle horn, and slapped the freed animal. He watched him lope away toward Railhead, and smiled easily. Mark's horse would be home by dawn.

Jack had corralled another horse, saddled, bridled, and tied him in a little sheltered gully about a quarter mile from the buildings before he slipped up into his own hayloft and lay back on the fragrant, cured timothy, and let the vivid scenes of the last fifteen hours run thoughtfully through his mind.

He was still pondering the devastating course of events when he heard the loft ladder creek under weight and rolled farther into the hay and watched with his gun cocked and ready. Slowly a battered, sweaty Stetson emerged through the hole in the floor and Will Olds's figure emerged.

"Jack?" It was little more than a whisper.

"Over here, by the Jackson fork."

The marshal came over, dropped wearily into the hay, and shoved his hat back with a sigh. "Man! One more night like this an' I'm goin' to sell out an' go to herdin' sheep." He looked closely through the soft darkness at Cole. "Just like I figured it. Kennedy's four gun hawks have the whole damned town stirred up. It didn't take much, though, not after that banker an' his brother got through blastin' you for all manner of a scoundrel."

"Just who is Kennedy, an' what is this all about?"

Olds leaned back and stuck a fragrant stalk of hay in his mouth. "It's like this. Some *hombre* hereabouts is goin' by the name o' Dodge Kennedy. The government knows there ain't no such man, y' see, 'cause we've checked every damned territorial list there is. Anyway, whoever Kennedy is, he's smugglin' guns to the Mexicans south o' the line, an' whiskey he gets from the Mexicans north to the reservation Injuns. Real nice *hombre*. If he's left alone, there'll be the damnedest revolution on both sides of the line you ever dreamed of. An'

34

Railhead'll be right in the middle of it with this mysterious Kennedy character settin' himself up as a sort o' dictator, or somethin'. Anyway, when he kept slippin' away from us, I sent Julie down to see if she could make him fall for her by playin' like she was a gal on the dodge."

For a long moment the marshal stopped talking and sucked on the hay stalk in silence, then he shook himself slightly and went on. "It worked a little too well, Jack. Somehow, Kennedy got suspicious o' her an' she ran for it." He shrugged. "You came in when you found her an' took her to your ranch. I reckon Kennedy had his Injun trackers foller an' then, when they found her, they waited until she was alone an' . . . an' . . . ."

"Yeah," Jack said softly. "Yeah. I can guess the rest. But there's another angle that's worryin' me. Why in hell's there such a big passel of Railhead men want me hung?"

Olds nodded his head. "That's easy. In the first place, Kennedy's sent gun hawks here to inflame the local cowhands. In the second place, he thinks you might've gotten Julie to talk, see? You've got to die, accordin' to Kennedy, for safety's sake."

Jack nodded in silence. It all made a pattern, a gruesome, grisly pattern that had spelled death for a girl. An idea dawned on him. He sat up suddenly. "Will, have you met Clem Miller? Little, sour-looking cuss who runs the livery barn at Railhead? The banker's brother?"

Olds nodded. "Yeah, he's the *hombre* who found the girl hangin' in your house."

"Clem's never been in my house before an' wouldn't have come in, either. He knows I've never had any use for him. When he went into the house, he *knew* I wasn't home, an' he *knew* what he'd find. I'll lay you odds, too, that he was the actual murderer."

Olds snapped his fingers and stood up. "That's it, Jack, fits like a glove. Listen, this banker's one of the lads who's been stirrin' folks up against you. I couldn't figger it at first. Now I can. He an' his brother are tied in with Kennedy. Maybe the brother killed Julie, like you think. He could've easily enough." He started toward the loft ladder. "Come on, cowboy, we're ridin'!"

The whiskey-inspired fury of the night before had died into a sour, dull lethargy. Railhead's inhabitants, and the cowboys, were gone. The town lay, dead and ghostly, in the watery, eerie moonlight when Will Olds, very tired-looking, and Jack Cole left their horses down a dark little alley and stalked forward afoot. Will nudged the rancher and made a bitter face. "I can still smell the brimstone."

Jack nodded understandingly and ducked down a twisted, warped little side street.

Olds frowned. "Where you goin'?"

"To see a banker I know."

Olds nodded grimly with a savage smile.

Jack crept up to a large, white, two-story house, the most pretentious home in Railhead. The marshal squeezed his arm as they slid into the black shadows of a gnarled old cottonwood tree. "Lights inside. Someone's up."

Jack nodded and went forward beckoning. They were up beside the house in a moment and could hear the indistinguishable mutter of voices coming from behind the closed window. Jack raised up, swore at the drawn blind, and slipped around the house until he found an open window. In silent triumph, he and the marshal crawled into the room, which turned out to be a large, garish bedroom, and lay on the floor, guns drawn, listening.

"I think he did, Dan. Anyway, we can't take any chances."

Dan Morgan's voice rose in a shrill whine. "No, Claude! She's my daughter! You can't!"

Miller's snarl of a laugh floated gratingly to the listening men. "Oh, can't I? Listen, Dan, you old fool, you've outlived your usefulness, too. You've gotten so damned jumpy lately folks have been wonderin' about it. Even Jack Cole asked me about you. If you think for a minute I'll endanger all I've built up for the past three years because of you an' your daughter. . . ."

Olds's voice hissed in Jack's ear: "Kennedy. Claude Miller's Kennedy." He pushed himself off the floor.

Jack grabbed him and felt the shaking fury in his taut muscles. "Where you going?"

"To kill the skunk, where'd ya think? I'm going to give him something for Julie, the son-of-a-bitch."

"No. Beth's in there. Maybe the whole damned crew."

He leaped up desperately and lunged for the marshal, but Olds was already outside the room, tiptoeing down the corridor closer to the big parlor where the voices came from, more distinctly now. Jack darted after Will, his gun out and cocked. The marshal threw off the rancher's hand outside the door and Jack recoiled from the fury that glittered like sparks from the marshal's hooded eyes.

Jack only had the tiniest glimpse of the blindingly lighted room as Will Olds, a wild cry rolling out of the constriction of his throat, flung open the door and opened fire. He saw Beth and Dan Morgan tied to chairs with Claude and Clem Miller sitting at a big oaken table. There were two other men standing over against the wall. Will's first blast of death crumpled one of these strangers in the midst of the man's pop-eyed look of horror and surprise, then the world seemed to explode into flaming guns and writhing bodies.

Jack got a momentary flash of Clem Miller's head mushrooming into a scarlet sunburst of gore and he saw Olds pump another shot into the broken body before Clem hit the table and slid off. He

caught the flash of a gun in Claude Miller's fist and fired on the upcurve. Miller looked at him through the thunderous, acrid stink of death and gunpowder. He let the hammer fall again. Miller sat down on his chair with a foolishly amazed expression in his eyes, then slid sideways. The noise stopped and Jack felt a sickening dizziness gushing up from inside. He looked down and saw the flapping half of his shirt drenched in blood over the ribs. Unconsciously he tried to tuck it in, then someone was holding him so tightly his broken ribs screamed and writhed and he fought clear, gasping.

"Jack! Oh, darling! You're hit!"

Will Olds looked over from where he was slashing at Dan Morgan's bounds. His face was a deathly gray and the fire that had blazed so crazily from his hooded eyes was dead ashes. He tried to force a smile, couldn't, and spoke into the sudden, awful silence: "Ma'am, that's the understatement of the year. He's butchered!"

That was the last thing Jack Cole remembered until he opened his eyes and saw Beth bending over him. Without looking any farther, he puckered up his lips and looked expectantly into her black eyes. There was a suspicious hint of moistness in them as her face came down and drained the fever out of him with a cool, crushing kiss that seemed to burn its way into his very soul. Dimly he heard a dry voice speaking and recognized it as belonging to U.S. Marshal Will Olds.

"All right, Dan. I don't think he's so interested in hearing how Miller, alias Dodge Kennedy, forced you to carry messages to his smuggler pals, after all." There was a dry snort. "Of course, if you'd failed and Miller'd killed your daughter like he'd threatened, well, he wouldn't be kissin' her now, would he?"

That did it. Before Dan Morgan could answer, Jack pulled away from Beth's moist, hot lips and looked at the two men. "Is that the story, Dan? He actually was going to kill Beth if you didn't play ball with him?"

Dan Morgan's old face was still drawn and sick-looking. He nodded. "Yes. And he was fixin' to rob the bank an' clear out when he sent Clem out to your ranch to kill that little girl. Said things were gettin' too hot around Railhead an' he'd clean out and leave."

Jack was looking in fascinated horror at Beth's father when Olds spoke. "That about finishes the thing, Jack." His brooding, hooded eyes had a sick, haunted look. "By the way, Julie an' I were engaged." His face swung toward Beth. "Would you do something for me, Beth? Would you sort of see that her grave's kept from the grass an' weeds, an' put flowers on it for me until I can get back, every once in a while?" All three of them heard the sudden, awful choke in his voice.

Beth couldn't speak. She looked at the marshal and nodded. He turned with a lonely nod to them

all and walked out of the room. Beth fell across Jack's chest with agonized little sobs shaking her body in deep anguish. He reached up with one hand and stroked her black hair as old Dan tiptoed out of the room and softly closed the door.

Longhorn Trail

I

They were strung out for miles, a reddish brown serpentine of broad backs blandly pacing the summertime range, looking deceptively lethargic and harmless despite their wicked long horns that swept straight out sometimes two feet, then sharply tilted at the outer ends. It was not unusual for those horns to reach a span of four feet, and a six-foot span was not unheard of. With hooks like that longhorn cattle could pick up a mounted man, disembowel his horse, and hurl them both ten feet away to be churned to a red froth by sharp hoofs.

Wolves, the bane of calving grounds, rarely pulled down longhorn calves, and the cows with small calves were more dangerous than the bulls. In fact, they were more dangerous than a she-bear with young because a she-bear had poor eyesight and charged by scent, but a longhorn cow could see movement a mile off in the dusk, and, when she charged, there was small chance of ducking clear for she was as light and quick on her feet as a doe deer.

The bulls would fight anything that offered to stand. When there were no wolves or bears, they'd fight one another. And it was a poor longhorn that couldn't jump a five-foot windfall tree with room to spare, or swim a mile-wide river, shake once, and rush at the nearest man on foot. They seldom

went out of their way to attack mounted men, but a man on foot in the path of a big drive was doomed, for no man living could outrun or outmaneuver a longhorn.

They were called Texas cattle, but actually they'd originated in Mexico, inbreeds and throwbacks to the early-day Spanish cattle. They were a breed apart and it took a special breed of men to handle them. They would drag through the killing heat of a blistering midsummer day, and, when everyone was certain they were exhausted, a sudden clap of thunder could start a stampede that wouldn't end for twenty miles and perhaps ten hours. A man inadvertently hunting kindling for his supper fire coming face to face with one in the buckbrush had a short moment to utter a prayer, then, if he didn't manage somehow to elude the critter, he'd get skewered.

They were wicked and pig-eyed, slab-sided and razor-backed. They had not the brains God gave a goose, could outrun a good horse, jump as high and squat as low. They were sometimes speckled or spotted or marked with patches of white, but more often *moreno*—brown.

The only reason anyone suffered them at all was because in Texas they brought $1 a head but up in Kansas on the plains where the railroad tracks extended they brought $75 a head. They were tough meat, to be sure, but they were plentiful; there was a voracious Yankee meat market, so there were men

who would go through all the anguish and peril of driving them that infernal distance.

But like the land of the Southwest itself, long-horns molded their handlers into a separate kind of men, very different from any other kind of cowman. In the Northwest they were called cowboys, but not in the Southwest; there they were *vaqueros*, which in Mexican or Spanish meant about the same thing, but there was a difference. A cowboy could be anyone. All a man had to know to be a cowboy was to spread his legs and haul a horse between them. A *vaquero*, as Jess Howard once said, had to think like a longhorn, act like a horse, fight like a Comanche, and be as tough as a cactus apple.

Jess Howard should have known. He'd been taking herds up the Longhorn Trail for fourteen years. When he made his first drive, he'd been twelve years old. He was an old men at twenty-four, wise and seasoned and weather-burned. He could smell Comanches two miles off and could tell a horse thief just by looking at him. He also knew the signs of the heavens, the disposition of the longhorns, and the nature of men. He'd broken a leg in a stampede that had held him off the trail for one year, and he'd been shot with a *bois d'arc* arrow that had held him back another year, but Jess Howard, at twenty-six, was back again with a tough crew and a thousand head, the aggregate gather of four Texas ranches. He had a little sack

of gold coins in his bedroll, the blessings of the people who'd hired him to take their critters to the Kansas plains, and a good head start over other drovers, because one thing he'd learned years back was the first herd up the trail, come springtime, got the best price in Kansas.

Most trail bosses took two or three wagons. Not Jess Howard. He used one wagon for the *cocinero* and everything else was either tied behind his men's cantles or was left behind. "You travel light," he told the men when he hired them on, "and you travel fast. If you live to reach Kansas, you'll draw forty a month, which is twenty more'n you'd draw buckin' brush down in Texas gathering cattle. Once you start out with me, there'll be no turnin' back and no unnecessary stopping."

If any man had doubted that hard talk, by the time the herd hit the red-bark country he knew a damned sight better; when Jess Howard said there'd be no unnecessary delaying, he meant exactly that.

They were intercepted by Mexican brigands just before leaving the bottoms of the Red River. Jess had mustered all hands—six Texans and himself, lined them out on the west side of the herd, and made a charge. The Mexicans discreetly withdrew. There had been twenty of them.

At the Bravo they'd encountered migrating Comanches, and that was a stickier situation because the Comanches never ran from anything

or anyone. Jess had curled his skinny long legs under him, puffed the pipe, and gravely handed over a sack of sugar and two beeves. If the boys drank their coffee unsweetened, at least they were above ground to drink it.

Beyond the Bravo they hit the thunder country. It was rough and tilted, craggy and wild. Thunderstorms hung out there later in the white-hot summers. The object was to get through it before that time of year because all it took to scatter a thousand flighty-brained, murderous longhorn cattle was a good clap of thunder. Especially at night was this dangerous for the stupid brutes couldn't be depended upon to flee *away* from the strong sweat scent of men. Many a *vaquero* had been trampled to red jelly right in his sougan while sound asleep.

But Jess took them through the thunder country without incident, too. He swam the Sangre de Cristo with them. It was named that by old-time Spanish explorers because in each swollen spring-time red clay mud far upriver colored the water nearly scarlet. Blood of Christ, the Spaniards had named it, but many a Texas man who couldn't swim—and blessed few could—called it far worse names, because, if his saddle horse floundered, he drowned.

But they got across the Sangre, too, without inci-dent, or, as Harper Ellis said one evening at supper with his big shoulders comfortably settled against

the wagon's forewheel, his ugly bronzed face impassively set: "When a feller gets past all the worst things, he falls to wonderin' . . . just what the devil is up ahead. There's got to be something. Ain't no drive I ever even heard of before come this far without serious trouble."

The cook—called their *cocinero* after the custom of bilingual border Texans—had an answer for Harper Ellis. He was older than any of them—forty—and crippled in both legs from being dragged nearly to death by a runaway green colt. His name was Jonathan Little, which, in humorous moments, the others teased him with by reversing it. "The Lord," he solemnly told them around their little supper fire, "looks out for Texans, babies, and drunks."

John Ewell Brown—called Jeb because those were his initials—said: "He didn't do too good a job last year, Jonathan. You recollect Billy Hays? Well, I was right there at Tularosa when a greaser threw a knife in a crowded saloon and it went up to the hilt in Billy's back. That was with a Goodnight drive."

Jonathan, irascible and bull-headed, would not be vanquished that easily, and especially by Jeb Brown who was half his age, the pup of the Howard crew. "Well, dang it all, you got to figure the Lord's goin' to whittle 'em down once in a while. Otherwise, there'd be more Texans than anyone else an' that wouldn't do, would it?"

Jeb poured the dregs from his tin cup and innocently said: "Why? What'd be wrong with that? Ain't no better people, are there? Besides, if there weren't Texas men to take the beef up to Kansas, think of all the Yankees that'd starve."

"Let 'em," growled the dark, lean man with the saber scar across his left cheek whose black eyes more often than not glowed with a strange bitterness, sitting next to Jess Howard. His name was Potter Houston; some said he was distant kin to the great Texas patriot, Sam Houston (who'd been called by the Indians "Big Drunk"). "There's too many damned Yankees anyway."

Jess Howard sopped grease from his tin plate with sourdough bread, set the plate aside, and licked his fingers. Potter Houston, he knew, had acquired that saber gash at Sabin Pass while serving with the 10th Texas Cavalry against invading Union forces during the war. "There may be too many," Jess said, "but it's their cartwheels that pay for the cattle, so I'm in favor of 'em breedin' like rabbits."

Potter mused a moment, then said: "But we whittled 'em down a mite, years back. We whittled 'em down all right."

The others fell silent. They, too, recalled that war. Worse, they recalled its aftermath when the vengeance of a wrathful victor had been turned loose to ravish and pillage. But for every Potter Houston who lived with his memories, there were a hundred others who were willing to forget and move ahead into the future of a reunited land with the prosperity that had belatedly come. The trouble was, up in Yankee-loving Kansas where victor and vanquished came face to face every livelong day, men like Potter Houston could, and very often did, start the shooting all over again.

It was black Gabriel who smoothed things over at the supper fire. Gabriel was the color of a moonless night. He'd been born a slave, but after emancipation he'd taken to the trail as other blacks also did. Not many, because it was in most ways a harder life than slavery had ever been, but a few, and they were accepted by Texans, their color notwithstanding, for Texas men admired courage, resourcefulness, and loyalty, regardless of the color of a man's hide. They didn't discriminate, although years later folks would say they did. At least they didn't discriminate because of a man's color. They *did* discriminate against timid men, black or white, or troublesome men, or thieves and liars. But not against black *vaqueros* just because they were black.

Gabriel said: "Mistah Jess is plumb right. A Yank is a Yank, an' his money's as good as anyone else's. We don't got to like 'em or even live amongst 'em, jes' take their money and feed 'em Texas beef." Then Gabriel said: "One time I knew a real fine one. I took his boots."

The others looked at Gabriel, waiting. All but Jeb

Brown knew Gabriel was laying a trap. Jeb walked right into it. He said: "Well, didn't he put up no fight?"

"No, sir," answered Gabriel. "I jes' tol' you . . . he was a real fine Yankee. He was a dead one."

They all laughed. Jeb looked down into his empty plate and growled under his breath.

Their humor was like that; it had to be; their life was hard. Each dawn could be their last day on earth. They went everywhere armed and lay down at night with no guarantees. They'd matured in a war-ravaged land, had cut their teeth on gun barrels, had survived the high scream of Comanche raiders, flashfloods that dumped thirty inches of water in a single night, had baked under venomous summer suns, had looked Mexican marauders in the eye a hundred times without blinking before achieving maturity, and asked nothing more than to be free men in their wild world. The meek among them did not live long enough to cast much of a shadow. They and the Lord shared a reasonable confidence. He knew, and they also knew, a Texan could not possibly reach maturity if he tried to keep the Fifth Commandment. *Thou shalt not kill.* They killed to survive, so that the things they believed in could survive, they and the Lord knew how this was, how it had to be, and for that reason they enjoyed an easy familiarity, one with the other.

But beyond the borders of Texas other people

viewed them differently. They feared and often despised Texans. They kept their daughters inside when Texas drovers passed their Kansas towns; they kept their guns loaded and their best saddle stock safely corralled. They sighed with prodigious relief when the last dust settled. They considered the Texans in the identical light that they considered the devil—essential evils, necessary white Indians who brought their vicious longhorns up the torturous miles because no one else had the guts or the foolhardiness even to make the attempt, and meat was at a premium on the plains where in one generation the mounted butchers had wiped out a hundred thousand buffalo, and there was only Texas beef to fill the gap.

Charley Goodnight had said it: "On our side, we feed 'em and take their money. On their side, they sell us whiskey and hate our guts."

Old Shanghai Pierce, tall as a tree in his stocking feet and bull-voiced, a transplanted Yankee turned Texan, had put it more forcibly. "They need us like they need sin, but they're so god-damned sanctimonious about both it makes a feller want to puke to listen to 'em."

Jess Howard's only philosophy, less colorful but infinitely more realistic, was: "Deliver the herd, get the cash, go back and make up another drive. It's the longhorns that are going to pull Texas up out of the poverty the war left her in. If there's bad feeling, don't let it interfere because we *lost* the

54

war. Just keep your sentiments to yourselves and take all the Yankee money you can get." And Jess tolerated no troublemaking on the trail when they finally got up to those Kansas towns. He was tough enough to make it stick, too. Even battle-scarred Potter Houston didn't cross Jess Howard.

II

The last man Jess had hired back in the brush country had been a man named Wayne Levitt. In a trade where nearly all the professionals knew every other *vaquero*, if not always by sight then at least by name and supper fire sagas, Wayne Levitt was a stranger. The reason Jess had hired him had been elemental. Wayne wore his gun as only men wore them who were thoroughly familiar with their use. He wore his boots and spurs and hat the same way, and he rode a center-fire A-fork Texas saddle atop a leggy bay horse built for speed and endurance and cow savvy.

The fact that Wayne Levitt had very little to say, stayed pretty much to himself, and missed nothing with his pale eyes as they moved upcountry didn't detract either, for his kind of a range-bred man was worth his weight in Yankee gold on a drive. It had been Levitt who'd spotted those migrating Comanches south of the thunder country by the Bravo River. It had also been Wayne Levitt who'd outshouted Potter Houston with his Rebel yell when they'd charged those Mexican marauders. But he was a loner. Even old Jonathan Little didn't scold Wayne Levitt like he did the others, because there was something about the way he ran a sidelong glance up and down a man that smelled of trouble. He was one of those quiet men who could chill folks to the marrow with his eyes. But he could also laugh, although not often because he seldom found anything to be very funny. But when they swam the Sangre de Cristo and black Gabriel's skittish mustang had come within an ace of dunking the black *vaquero*, and Gabe had howled like a banshee with the whites of his eyes rolling heavenward in sincere appeal, Wayne had howled in glee even as he'd taken down his rawhide reata to flick a loop out in case Gabe slipped from the saddle. Gabe had hung on like grim death and had later on tumbled to the dry earth as shaken as a non-swimmer gets after surviving a near drowning, so Wayne hadn't had to rope him to save his life. It had amused them all— excepting, of course, Gabe—and it had been the first time they'd seen Wayne Levitt laugh.

But aside from that one incident, Wayne hadn't laughed again. A couple of times he'd grinned, like the frosty morning when Potter had stepped up over leather and had opened his rein hand a second later to find it full of grass. The horse had bucked him from the cold saddle so fast and hard Potter had never even found both stirrups before he was belly down on the ground. It was the kind of humor they all understood, so they accepted Levitt, even as they also wondered a little about him. After all, they were a long way from home or from Kansas. There was nothing else to wonder about.

"Damned outlaw on the run," muttered Jonathan to Jess the day they halted near a saltlick to rest the herd. "You watch him. He never sets down without his back's protected, an' his eyes never stop moving. He sees everything. An' that tied-down gun he wears. I tell you, Jess, you hired on a ringer this time."

Howard's drawled reply was matter-of-fact. "I'd hire Wild Bill Hickok and Jesse James if that's what it'd take to deliver the herd onto the plains, Jonathan. Quit stewing about it. He's a good man with the herd. That's all you 'n' I've got to worry about."

Black Gabe seemed to be Wayne Levitt's favorite among the men. They shared tobacco and sometimes even rode along side-by-side conversing. But when Jonathan nosily tried to get it out of Gabe what they talked of, Gabriel would roll his eyes and shake his head.

But there was no friction. Wayne Levitt carried his share of the work, stayed mostly to himself, and gave none of them any reason to chouse him. Still, they wondered, and once or twice Potter or Jeb or Jonathan would try to draw him out. They never succeeded.

It took thirty days to make the midway mark, which was a huge grassy prairie with a sluggish creek bisecting it. There was a huge old black oak growing all by itself out in the middle of the plain. Invariably that's where camp was pitched. It was custom to let the herd grass up in this place, because the next fifty miles were over shale-rock shallow ground that grew only sparse and sickly grass.

That old tree had initials and pungent remarks carved all over its rough bark. There were even some cordial insults whittled there from some rider who'd headed up the trail to some friend who'd come up with another drive. They called this place Black Oak Prairie. It was here they ran into their first serious trouble.

The weather was perfect, bland, and warm with little ground swell breezes passing along. The feed was tall enough to have good strength to it, and the creek hadn't yet got that green scum along its low banks that it would acquire later on after full summertime came.

Jonathan brought forth two poles on the sundown side of his wagon, set them into the ground, then drew half the wagon canvas over the poles forming a protective, shady place where he worked. It was from under this texas, as it was called, that Jonathan spotted the horsemen more than a mile out, sitting their saddles eyeing the camp. Old Jonathan, who'd had his share of brushes with

Indians, beat the bottom of a dented old stew pan, which brought the others loping in from a mile out westerly where they were gauging the drift of the herd, and, when Jess rode up, he pointed.

"Damned redskins," he growled. "Look at 'em sittin' out there like statues studyin' us to see how strong we are an' whether they'd dare make a run on us."

With the dazzling sunlight brightening everything to a brassy brilliance it was difficult to make out much more at that distance other than that those far-off strangers were mounted men, and that of course went without saying; there were no unmounted men abroad in a country as flat as this, for to be afoot was to be totally at the mercy of anyone who came along, and there was no law. Not this far from anywhere. Armed, mounted men ruled this grassland empire. If they liked what they saw, they took it—if they could. First, of course, they reconnoitered, which seemed to be exactly what those strangers were doing now.

"Not Indians," Wayne Levitt said after a long, hard look. "Whites."

Jonathan screwed up his eyes for a better look. "How can you be sure?" he demanded. "Look like damned red devils to me."

"They got hats on," answered Levitt, "and you can see the reflection of sunlight off their upended carbine butts. Whites or Mexicans. And I don't think they're greasers . . . not this far north."

Jess dismounted, walked to the rear of the wagon, rummaged a moment, then drew forth a battered old brass spyglass. He pulled the thing out to its full length and set it to his right eye. For a long while he stood there, peering.

Jonathan's patience gave out. "Well," he barked peevishly, "you goin' to study 'em all day . . . or what?"

Jess lowered the glass but kept peering out across the dazzling intervening distance. "Whites, all right. Ten or twelve of them. They're armed to the teeth and look pretty rough."

Potter Houston nodded his head grimly. "Comancheros!" he exclaimed. "White renegades who trade an' live with the Comanches. You sure there's that many, Jess?"

Howard strolled over and held up the spyglass. "Look for yourself. There's a bushy-bearded feller out in front a little ways. Take a good look at him. If he's not a cut-throat, I'll eat my hat."

Potter looked a long time. He handed the glass to Gabe who, also, looked. Jeb had the last long look because Wayne Levitt waved the glass away as he said: "Nothing to worry about as long as it's broad daylight." He stepped down off his horse and soberly glanced at Jess. "They'll hit the herd tonight, sure."

Potter swore. "Not if we hit them first, they won't, eh, Jess?"

Jonathan spoke up quickly, giving Jess no

60

chance to answer Potter. "Listen, I been around long enough to know something about those renegade devils, an' I can tell you from experience that, if there's ten or twelve of 'em sittin' out there lettin' us see 'em bold as brass, there's more of 'em skulkin' around somewhere else . . . unless they got some bronco Comanches ridin' with 'em, which amounts to the same thing."

Jess took back his spyglass, raised it, and studied the distant, motionless horsemen once more. Then he pushed the spyglass back into itself and spat into the dust. Here was trouble. Comancheros often stampeded herds, then drove off as many as they could, and afterward trailed their stolen stock up to Kansas for a one hundred percent profit. And they would fight; only fools ever claimed Comancheros were skulkers and cowards. No one, white, black, brown, or red who lived with the Comanches for any length of time at all was a coward.

He went back to the rear of the wagon, put the glass away, and slowly paced back to the others. It was one thing to charge a band of Mexican marauders who outnumbered you three to one, and it was something altogether different to charge Comancheros, even though the odds against you were considerably less. There had to be a third way.

Giving them a few head as he'd done with the Indians weeks before wouldn't suffice. Talking them out of raiding the fanned-out herd would only be a waste of breath. Buying them off, even using all the gold he had in that little doeskin bag inside his bedroll, wouldn't work, either, for they'd know they could get that gold anyway, if they chose to attack for it.

He looked briefly at the sky, then said: "Jonathan, how's supper coming?"

The cook looked at him as though he'd suddenly lost his mind. "It's coming," he answered. "What the hell, it's only half afternoon, Jess."

"Well, maybe we'll eat a little early. You other fellers, off-saddle but tie your horses to the wagon. Wayne? You care to make a little sashay out and around for maybe an hour or so?"

Levitt nodded. If he hadn't understood what an early supper had to do with their dilemma, at least he understood the purpose of making a scout. He turned and rode off westerly, in the opposite direction from those distant mounted men. The others dismounted and yanked off their rigging, dumped saddles, bridles, booted carbines nearby Jonathan's texas, and stood around. Gabe called softly to say the distant watchers were pulling out. Everyone stepped forth to see. There was nothing very spectacular about that abrupt departure. Evidently the Comancheros had seen all they needed to see—seven drovers, one wagon, and a thousand head of longhorns. Depending upon their intention and their number, it could be an ideal situation for them.

"Sure would like to drop a bullet among 'em," murmured Gabriel, making no move to do anything like that at all. "I've met up with them kind before. They's worse'n wolves. Worse even than Indians. Them's pure Texas scum."

No one contradicted Gabe. Even young Jeb, who'd never before seen Comancheros up close, had heard enough tales about them to make his hair bristle. As the crowd of leisurely riders dropped away far out, Jeb said: "Jess, it's botherin' me. What's an early supper got to do with them?"

"Yeah," muttered old Jonathan. "I'd like to know that, too."

Jess went over into the shade of the texas and said: "We can't hit 'em like we offered to do with the Mexicans, and can't smoke a pipe like we did with the Comanches. So . . . we eat early. Then, after Wayne gets back and reports where they're making for, we slip away after nightfall and do our damnedest to hit their camp before they hit ours."

Potter Houston smiled. Gabe rolled his eyes. Jeb stood silently thoughtful. Only Jonathan Little had a comment to offer. "If they got the same notion, there's a right fair chance we're going to slip past each other in the dark."

"Not you," Jess said. "You're going to stay right here, keep the fire going, and make enough small noises so they'll think all of us are here." Jonathan wrinkled up his brow and opened his mouth to protest. Jess didn't give him a chance. "They'll have a spy lyin' out there in the grass, watching everything we do. After the rest of us slip away, Jonathan, maybe that spy'll pull back, too, in the dark. But whether he does or not, you fool him for all your worth, and, if things work out, I'll fetch you back a topknot."

Jonathan cursed and shook his head and fell to work angrily preparing supper, but he argued no more, which meant he would co-operate.

III

Wayne Levitt came back shortly before sundown, leading his horse and carrying a stick he used as a sort of cane. He'd been afoot a long time, he told the others as he handed his mount to Jeb and sat down under the texas to let off a big sigh. He stated that walking for any distance on his spindly legs was a virtue he'd been denied extracting any pleasure from since birth. Jonathan handed him a cup of black coffee. As he sipped this, he pointed with his chin, Indian fashion, southwest.

"They've got a camp at the far edge of the prairie in a cane brake where there are some rocks."

"How many?" Potter Houston asked, and leaned forward to be certain he heard the answer correctly.

"Just the bunch you saw," Wayne answered. "Ten or twelve. But they've got some Comanche ponies in a faggot corral down there next to a water hole, so I'd guess they know where the redskins are, if they need help."

"What else they got down there?" asked Harper Ellis.

"Injun teepees and a couple of old brush shelters. The camp looks to me like one of those old-time sites where the redskins used to camp while on a hunting trip."

Potter and Gabe exchanged a look and a little nod. They were both pleased to learn there wasn't a whole additional band of enemies camped beyond on the prairie.

"How far's the camp?" asked Jess.

"Six, eight miles, and, by God, I had to hoof it most of the way because the land's so cussed flat they'd have spotted me sure had I ridden it. I got blisters on my blisters. I never could understand why anyone'd have the gall to say walking's good for a man."

Jonathan, stirring a greasy stew in a copper pot over their small fire, said, cocking an eye at the darkening heavens: "All right, fetch your plates."

Levitt looked over at Jess, then on over at Jonathan. They hadn't eaten this early before. Jess understood the quizzical expression and explained what he had in mind.

Levitt listened without batting an eye, then went with the others to the chuck box on the side of the wagon for his eating utensils. He still said nothing as they lined up for Jonathan's serving. But later, as they were all seated in lengthening dusk, he shook his head. "This here is a two-way road. Unless we start right soon, even before it's safe to do so, they're going to be coming over this way."

Gabe said: "A feller don't often have much cause to be happy he was born black, but tonight us is goin' to be happy about it." He grinned, showing perfect white teeth. The others smiled back and Jonathan chuckled as he watched them eat. "I figure you fellers are goin' to need more'n just dumb luck," he went on. "You're goin' to need *puha*."

Puha was the Comanche word for personal power: luck, magic, extra good fortune. Every man was born with some *puha*, but no man ever knew for a fact just how good his power was until his life depended upon it.

Jess finished eating and swabbed out his plate with a swath of bent grass. He gulped down the coffee, dregs and all, got up, and went over to yank forth his carbine. The others finished, also, and got their guns. Jeb had to go to the back of the wagon and delve into a box for extra ammunition. The other, older men never went anywhere without wearing full cartridge belts; that was one of the basic differences between young and not-so-young Texans.

The sky was turning dark. Stars shone and a little scimitar moon was up there, its light about as powerful as diluted milk. Jonathan got his carbine, too.

He leaned it against the wagon and walked away from the little fire. If he and some skulking Comanchero were going to share the ensuing hours amid all the dark and hushed loneliness of this huge dead world, then Jonathan was going to have every advantage he could devise.

"Take care," Jess told him. "Little Jonathan you take care, hear?"

Jonathan made a sniffing sound for answer. He stood off a little distance and watched them head for their horses. He'd faced his share of dangers. Anyway, that spy probably had already started back to the Comanchero camp. It was now too dark to see a hundred yards ahead anyway.

They rode away at a careful walk, Wayne Levitt leading. There was a sweetness to the night air, a warm pleasantness that came from green grass and cooling earth below, and a cloudless, enameled sky above. It was a beautiful night. In other places men and girls were strolling hand in hand. But not within a hundred miles of Black Oak Prairie. There, death accompanied six silent men on their southeasterly course.

For an hour Levitt held the lead, then he halted to get belly down and press his ear to the earth. He stayed like that for nearly five full minutes while the others sat and waited. Then he rolled over, nodded his head, and silently sprang back to his feet.

"Their horses are milling," he reported, having

caught the faint reverberations through the ground. "That likely means they're getting ready."

Jess stepped down. There wasn't a tree or a bush or a rock anywhere to tether their animals to. "Jeb," he said softly, "you're horse holder. Whatever happens, don't let the critters get loose. If we're set afoot down here, they'll hit the herd and probably get old Jonathan in the bargain."

Gabe, Jess, Potter Houston, and Wayne Levitt went ahead on foot. Levitt took the lead again until Potter suddenly came up even with him and stopped them with an upraised hand. Potter had ears like a lobo. After that, Levitt fell back to pace along with Gabriel and Potter Houston strode out ahead with Jess Howard five feet behind him. Harper Ellis came next.

The land began to dip and rise in little pock-like places. They encountered thrusts of granite that jutted up out of the sod like bones from a dyna-mited graveyard. A tangy, gamy scent came to them before they heard a horse softly nicker. That was when Potter dropped straight down. The others did likewise. They were not trying to avoid discovery so much as they sought to skyline the onward land.

Potter turned. "Wayne," he hissed. "How much farther?"

Wayne didn't answer. He raised a rigid arm pointing. Up ahead, backgrounded by the silver of paler light over upon the distant horizon, was a bulky shape of horse and rider. One of the Comancheros was already astride. They could see him looking over his shoulder back down where the camp lay, impatient for his companions also to get astride. The man had two bandoleers crossed upon his chest and was holding his carbine in his left hand. He was a perfect target as four guns silently came up out of the grass. He called something out in guttural Comanche, then in plain English he said: "Come along, dammit. We done wasted enough time as it is."

A high, grating voice answered from lower down, saying in an unmistakable Mexican accent: "Why hurry? They're lying under their wagon like frightened *muchachos*, waiting for us. We have plenty of time, *amigo*."

Potter Houston cocked his gun. That small sound traveled clearly to the mounted man. He whipped straight up and flung his head forward. Potter fired. Gabe fired. Wayne fired. Ellis fired. The Comanchero's horse collapsed and all hell broke loose. Four others ran up, yelling that they were under attack. Jess caught one over his sights and also caught another one. Potter sprang up with a keening yell and raced ahead. Right behind him Gabriel and Wayne Levitt also charged the camp. Mushrooming lancets of red flame sprang out at them. Jess Howard ran off to the left a little distance where he could see down into the breaks where the camp was. He raked the astonished men down there until his carbine went empty, then he dropped it and fired with his six-gun.

Someone, mortally hit down there where a dirty old teepee stood, ghostly pale and conical in the poor light, wailed and wailed as he threshed and heaved about upon the ground. Gabe caught that big-bearded man to one side while Wayne Levitt fired from the opposite side. The big man roared like an angry bull and took four shots before dropping to his knees. Then he fell over onto his face when another Comanchero, running blindly in panic, blundered into him. As the second one struggled to roll free and jump up. Potter Houston shot him from a distance of less than thirty feet right in the middle. The man cried out and drunkenly staggered backward. When he fell, two others turned to flee. Four guns swung on those two and cut them down ten feet apart.

Someone was yelling in both Spanish and English that he surrendered. Jess turned his gun in the direction of that voice and fired three times fast. The voice went abruptly silent. All Jess knew was that none of his men had been killed. He could see them moving, bent low in the darkness. Whether any had been injured or not he had no idea as he started running for that teepee. A man suddenly loomed up trying to get on a horse. Jess shot him in the side and he sprawled, freeing the horse that violently shied and turned tail to speed away. That was the last shot fired.

For a long time no one moved or spoke. Jess, close to the teepee, bent to scratch for fire and light the bottom of the tinder-dry old buffalo hide covering the teepee's sapling framework. As soon as the hide flared up, he ran back out where the others were, flung himself down in the grass, and waited. As soon as there was enough light to see by, he counted eight bodies crumpled here and there, broken and bloody and harmless. He lay perfectly still until the flames lighted up everything, then risked a call to Potter who was nearest.

"See any more?"

"Not a one," came back the short answer. "Just good ones . . . dead ones."

He called to others. "Gabe, Wayne, you boys see anything alive down there?"

The same answer came back from both the other Texans. But Gabe added something. "I heard horses runnin'. Them others must've run off, Mistah Jess."

That seemed probable, but all the same Jess called back for no one to move, for them all just to lie and wait until the flames died a little, before going in to investigate.

That took an hour, then they cautiously arose and went ahead. There were nine dead men, not eight, and for all the horses in the faggot corral there were only nine saddles. Three of the Comancheros had managed to escape into the southward night. But three renegades would not attack, so Jess's shrewd decision to hit first and hardest had saved the herd and perhaps their lives as well.

When they came together beside the faggot corral, he looked around. "Anyone hurt?" No one was. Wayne Levitt gave them one of his rare smiles.

"Good night's work," he said, perfectly satisfied. "But these lads got red-skinned friends. Those three'll head for the nearest Comanches. It'll be best for us to strike camp and get to hell out of here."

Jess strolled over to that bushy-bearded man, stripped off his cartridge-studded bandoleers, looped the things over his arm, and jerked his head. "Let's go. Jonathan'll get his souvenirs."

They stepped over the corpses and strode back to where the prairie leveled off again. Later, when they came upon young Jeb standing stiff as a ramrod with his carbine trained in the direction of their sounds, they whistled to let him know who it was.

Jeb was a trifle breathless. "Sounded like a reg'lar war," he said, watching the others test their *cinchas* before stepping up across leather.

Potter's answer to that was wry. "What do you know about what a war sounds like?"

They headed back and arrived south of the pale-topped wagon before 9:00. They hadn't actually been gone as long as it seemed. They dismounted, didn't see Jonathan, but paid that no mind, and

72

began off-saddling by the red, glowing low light of Jonathan's small, dying fire. They almost had their work done when the *cocinero* came hobbling in out of the westerly darkness, rifle hooked casually in the crook of an elbow. Jess turned and tossed Jonathan the bandoleers. "Off their leader," he said. "The bushy-faced big one."

"I'm right obliged," said Jonathan, pronouncing the last word as though it had two letters "e" where the letter "i" was. "I see none of you got hurt. How about them?"

"Plumb surprise," said Potter. "Nine dead, three missing. It was a good lick, Jonathan. Where was you? Lying low out there praying when you heard us coming?"

Jonathan said: "Somethin' like that. Not prayin', but I sure was hopin' it wasn't someone besides you boys." He kicked at the little fire. "I'll get the coffee to stewin' again. Fellers need a tonic afore they hit the sack after a strenuous night's work, I always say."

The men turned loose their animals and stacked their riggings. They made smokes and squatted by the fire, or they sat down with their backs to wagon wheels and simply gazed into the fire, but in either case they didn't say much. Men not often did, after a massacre like they had perpetrated. It was one thing to kill an individual, another thing altogether to see nine dead men sprawled lifelessly in the star shine. It sort of made men wonder, not especially about the finality of death, but rather at the brevity of life.

Jonathan got the tin cups and poured, then handed them around. Harper Ellis, the quietest among them since before the fight, now seemed for some reason to get a loose tongue after an hour of just sitting and gazing into the fire. "One time on the Brazos," he said, "I was ridin' point for a big gather, an' a bunch of redskins popped up outen an arroyo right in my face. M' heart liked to stop. Behind me eleven cowboys opened up, an' them Injuns just sort of all wilted right before m' eyes. I was petrified, I tell you, them bullets comin' from behind me like that, an' I never hardly even moved before it was all over. Afterward there lay them cussed Comanch' all over the place. We went around puttin' the hurt ones out of their misery an' I come onto this husky buck who'd been to mission school. I cocked my pistol and pointed it at his forehead an' he looks me plumb square in the eye an' says . . . 'We open our eyes and we are born, we close them and we are dead. It is a very short moment in between.' "

Jeb kept gazing at Harper after the others had looked away. "Well," he finally demanded. "Did you kill him, Harper?"

"Did I kill him? Well now, John Ewell Brown, that's a plumb stupid question. 'Course I killed him. He was an Injun, warn't he? What'd you expect me to do?"

"Well, nothing. . . ."

"Well, then, don't be askin' stupid questions."

Jess Howard flung away the grounds from his coffee cup and tossed the cup into Jonathan's wash bucket near the texas. He considered his stubby smoke, killed it against the earth, and heaved up off the ground slowly to turn completely around, looking and listening. "We'll pull out ahead of sunup tomorrow," he told them, "and keep moving until we're well out of this part of the country. I doubt if those three'll be able to round up enough broncos to hit us, but all the same a man's foolish to crowd his luck." The others nodded. "Jeb, you 'n' Potter take first watch. Good night."

The matter of bedding down was simple enough. A man kicked off his spurred boots, lay his guns beside his head, removed anything bulky from his pockets, deposited these things inside his hat, lay back upon his ground cloth, and closed his eyes. On a chilly night he drew a blanket atop him. On a night like that one, he just closed his eyes as Jess Howard did, and sleep came. Nine dead men might trouble a conscience here and there among Texas men, but not among Jess Howard's crew. They'd seen dead ones before. Anyway, it wasn't the dead ones you had to watch; it was the live ones.

IV

They trailed over crumbly shale for fifty miles. The grass was a sickly green and so short critters got dust in their noses trying to pick it. It was a bad contrast to Black Oak Prairie where the feed had been lush and ample. Furthermore, the cattle didn't like being pushed across it. For that matter the men didn't like leaving the prairie, either. Ordinarily they'd have camped there a week, maybe even ten days, resting foot-weary horses and tucked up cattle. That, at least, had been Jess Howard's plan, but those nine dead Comancheros had changed all that.

Water became a problem, too. They found some brackish potholes where seepage and rainwater had trickled in, but it wasn't fit for men to drink and the animals made faces after sipping it, too. It was sort of like gulping down thick chocolate.

Harper Ellis wrinkled his big, hooked nose and said he smelled trouble. Jess had no comment about that; he expected trouble, also, but it was better to ride along watching closely for the quarter it might come from, than poking along gloomily talking about it.

Fifteen miles was a good day's walk in flat country, but they kicked up powdery dust for three days across this shallow earth country and still couldn't see the end of it. Jess had made this crossing before so he knew about where they'd hit decent feed and water again. Potter Houston knew, also, for he'd made the same crossing, too. But knowing and doing were different things, and on the fourth day, when the bulls began fighting one another out of sheer irritability while the cows kept trying to cut back, Jonathan Little, up there on his wagon seat where he had a good view all around, sang out that there were riders far back.

Jess got his spyglass and looked. Afterward, when they nooned beneath a blazing, malevolent yellow sun, he told them those three Comancheros who'd escaped were probably among those riders far back. "Want their revenge, I reckon," he said. "Anyway, there's about twenty bronco bucks back there."

"Couple more days," observed Harper Ellis, "an' we'll run out of Comanch' territory. If they're going' to hit, they better do it right soon."

On the Longhorn Trail unexpected good fortune could surprise a man just the same as it could appear anywhere else on earth. Old Jonathan, returning to camp with a sack full of cow chips to feed into his little cooking fire, said: "Hey, maybe I was seein' things, but out there about a mile I swear I spotted some wagons bearin' southward."

The men looked astonished. "Wagons?" Potter said. "What're you talkin' about . . . wagons. Hell's bells, this isn't a wagon route, Jonathan."

The cook, squatting beside his fire for their noon

stew, turned grumpy. "Well, consarn you, Potter Houston, if you're fixin' to call me a liar, you'd better sashay out there and make positive you're dead right, first."

Potter wordlessly mounted up. So did Jess. They loped away from the wagon and through the gamy dust of a thousand disgruntled longhorns strung out far ahead for the nooning.

It *was* wagons. Thirteen of them all coupled up close and bearing southward exactly as Jonathan had reported. Potter's dourness came up as they sat their saddles, considering this phenomenon. "Damned greenhorn Yankee immigrants," he stated. "Look yonder, Jess. Strung out like this was settled Missouri and there wasn't a patch of trouble between here 'n' there."

Jess was less resentful and more interested. Texas was getting its share of settlers, but, as Potter had said before, the Longhorn Trail was no regular caravan route. Those trail ways were much farther east, over where the settlements lay about a day's travel apart. He turned in the saddle to gaze southward where the broncos were. They had faded back into the southerly distances, probably, he thought, to wait for nightfall.

Potter saw the thoughtful look on Jess's face and said: "We'd better lope on over and pass the warning. Yankees or not, they're likely to get their stock stampeded tonight by them cussed rene-gades."

What Potter left unsaid was that a stampede raid on the immigrants by those Comancheros and their friends couldn't help but also cause the longhorns to panic, too. In the night a thousand orry-eyed, savage-horned wild cattle charging blindly through the darkness could cause a lot of death and destruction.

Jess lifted his reins. They loped off westerly, heading for the distant wagons. For a half hour the only sound was the abrasive rub of dry saddle leather, then someone up ahead sang out in a loud cry of warning. They had been sighted by the wagoners.

Jess slowed to a fast walk. At his side Potter Houston's scarred face shone with greasy perspiration. His black eyes glowed with their habitual hardness. "Welcomin' committee," he muttered, and thrust with his chin in the direction of five riders loping away from the wagons toward them. "Figure we're renegades sure as the devil."

Jess reserved judgment until the oncoming armed men were close enough to make out clearly. One thing was immediately evident; those immigrants were not cattlemen. Farmers more than likely, from their dress and armament. They carried rifles, not carbines, and they wore the drab attire of people whose lives were spent in the service of the soil.

Jess halted to sit and wait. Potter wiped sweat off his swarthy face with a sleeve. The five outriders also slowed to a walk, using the intervening distance as an excuse to make an assessment of the pair of mounted Texans. There was a raw-boned, bearded older man leading them. As the five came up close and halted, it was this pale-eyed old patriarch who gravely nodded and said: "Good day to you, gentlemen. You must be the herders with those longhorns we spotted."

Jess spoke his name and introduced Potter Houston. The bearded, big old raw-boned man did the same with his companions. His name, he said, was Eli Young, and he was wagon master for his train that consisted of God-fearing farmers in search of new land and a fresh start. "Texas," he told Jess, "is said to have all we need." Then he said something that made Potter's dark eyes bitterly glow. "We're ex-soldiers with land warrants from the federal government given us under the Soldiers and Sailors Bounty Act."

Jess was about to mention the Comancheros, but Potter cut in first, saying: "Mister, you got your gall. Texas won't welcome you with a heap of friendliness."

Old Eli Young fixed Potter with his pale eyes and seemed to be taking Houston's measure. Eventually, crossing both big hands atop his saddle horn, he said quietly: "Mister Houston, what's past is past. If you have scars to show, so have we. An' if you folks down here want trouble, we can oblige you right well. Only it appears to us it's to the common benefit for us all to live civilized, now that the killing's done with. We got the same God, Mister Houston, an' we got the same heritage. We come to cause you no harm, an' we come here to take no harm from you."

Potter's saber scar got livid but Jess spoke out, cutting him off from forcing a fight. "Mister Young," he said. "A few days back we had a brush with Comancheros. I don't know whether you folks know what Comancheros are or not, but they're the worst kind of renegades down here. We left nine of them dead. A while back we spotted a mixed band of Indians and Comancheros following us. That's why we rode over here. To warn you to corral your wagons tonight and put all your livestock inside the wagon circle. They likely won't attack you if you're forted up, and, since we're ready for them, too, they might just sort of skulk and maybe try pickin' off a straggler now and then, or maybe run off some loose stock. The main thing is, I've got a thousand longhorns. They're edgy from bein' on short feed. If those renegades try for a stampede, it could raise hell with you and us."

One of the younger men with Eli Young, a burly, powerful man with a long-barreled musket balanced across the seat of his saddle, said: "What do you propose, Mister Howard? That we patrol between the two camps tonight?"

Jess nodded at that immigrant. "Something like

that. And to make certain you don't shoot us an' we don't shoot you in the dark, the pass word'll be . . . San Jacinto. All right?"

Eli Young stroked his grizzled beard and gazed out and around. "Maybe if we made a run on them, they'd leave," he said. "How do you feel about that, Mister Howard?"

"Not again, Mister Young. That's what we did a few nights back to kill nine of them. We can't catch them like that again. They're as sly as Indians and ten times as deadly."

"Indians," said a youthful immigrant, "don't fight at night."

Potter made a nasty laugh at that. "Yank, Comanche Indians *do* fight at night. They use a full moon for most of their big raids. Maybe your northern redskins don't like dyin' in the dark, but a Comanche'll spend the whole night crawlin' right up to split your skull. You folks've got a heap to learn about Texas, I can see that."

The immigrant men disliked Potter. It showed clearly in their faces. Jess was annoyed by Potter's noticeable contempt; they had enough enemies, natural and otherwise. If Providence had seen fit to provide him with these people right when he surely needed them, he wasn't about to permit Potter's bitterness to interfere.

He said to the immigrants: "That's true, men. Comancheros and the Comanches specialize in night fighting. But if we keep a close watch, we'll come through. What's troublin' me is that they might get around us and hit my herd. Unless they've seen your wagons, that'll still be their wish."

"And if they've seen our wagons?" asked Eli Young.

"Women and gold, livestock and your personal valuables," growled Potter. "They'd let the long-horns pass any day or night, Yank, to get their hands on them things."

Jess said: "They've seen your wagons by now, Mister Young. You can bet money on that."

Young looked around at his companions. They alternately looked back and gazed across at the pair of lanky, bronzed Texans. They seemed half inclined to believe, half inclined to doubt and wonder. Old Eli resolved their doubt by saying to Jess: "We'll ride back to your camp with you." Before anyone said any more, Eli turned to the burly, powerful man. "Paul, go back and pass the order to circle up with the livestock inside. Put the men on the alert and parcel out the night watches." The man called Paul turned his horse without a word and loped away.

Jess wheeled his mount and started back across the wide plain toward his own nooning camp. The immigrants had nothing to say, not even after they got a close look at the grazing longhorns, more cattle in one drive than any of them had ever seen before. They were a close-lipped group of men, wary-eyed and careful. Eli Young rode along like some old patriarch out of Biblical times, head up, great gray beard splayed and grizzled, pale, proud eyes endlessly moving, his work-hardened right hand balancing the musket across his lap. He was along in his years but sparse and oaken, a fit leader for his flock, no doubt, and in Jess's eyes the kind of rough zealot who turned his back on no trouble, or no supplicant.

When they reached the wagon, Jonathan and the other Texans came around to gaze at the strangers. This quiet interest was candidly returned. Jess led the immigrants to their little cow-chip fire and gave them coffee. It was cooler around here by the texas. Wayne Levitt went off to look for his horse but the other Texans stood idly around, looking and listening. It was an awkward meeting; these men had little in common and nothing to talk about except their common peril. When that topic was exhausted, they stood, dumb and awkward, considering one another.

The immigrants had thirteen wagons and twenty-two men capable of fighting. Including the Texas drovers there would be nearly thirty armed men to patrol back and forth between the wagon camp and the cow camp. Jess thought that was enough, providing the Comancheros and their bronco-buck friends didn't number many more. He looked around for Wayne Levitt to send him out on a scout. Someone said he'd walked off when the strangers rode up, so Jess sent Potter Houston to make the scout. Jeb or Harper Ellis could have just as well gone, but Potter's absence from the cow camp, at least as long as the Yankee settlers were there, would be a relief to Jess.

The plan they devised was simple. The men would ride back and forth in pairs. They had their password—San Jacinto, an historic name in Texas lore—and, if anyone got into serious trouble, he would fire his gun. That would be the signal for everyone to come on the run. It was a purely defensive plan, but Jess Howard said he thought they should give the renegades a chance to size up their enemies and maybe to pull out without any killing, if they would, because all either the immigrants or Texans wanted was to be left alone. Old Eli agreed and went back to his horse. His companions also mounted up. With quiet nods the immigrants turned and rode away. It was then close to 3:00 in the dazzling, hot afternoon.

V

Jonathan made leaden dumplings for their stringy stew and plenty of black java. He fed them early and said something about that, it being the second time in a short week they'd had chow in late afternoon instead of late evening.

"Next thing you know it'll be four meals a day instead of three, an', when that happens, I'll have to get more pay."

"For what?" Harper asked, sniffing the stew. "Throwing an extra sock into the stuff you got the gall to call food?"

Jonathan raised a wicked cleaver menacingly and Harper retreated.

Wayne Levitt strolled back. Jess eyed him but said nothing. Jeb and Gabe went gathering cow chips. It was a dull, hot afternoon with no more sightings of the renegades made at the cow camp. Potter returned just ahead of red sundown to report that he'd found no sign of the renegades beyond their tracks. "It looks to me like they got about as many men as we'll have. But if they went southward back the way they come, I sure couldn't see hide nor hair of 'em."

Levitt asked one question: "Barefoot horses?"

Every one of them understood the significance of that question. Whites, even renegade whites, did not ride barefoot horses. But Comanches did.

"Half and half," said Potter, off-saddling with his back to the others.

"Then there were more damned Comancheros," stated Levitt. "The bunch we hit was only part of the crew. The rest were probably at some redskin camp. That accounts for so many Comanches being with them now."

"I'd say that's about right," drawled Potter, dumping his equipment and striding over where Jonathan was dishing up his tangy stew. "I'd also say those Yankee settlers are our salvation, too.

Any renegade living, red or white, would turn away from a herd like ours to get a chance at all those wagons and teams and other valuables such folks pack along." Jonathan handed him a plate and a scowl. Potter ignored the look and went over under the texas into the shade to squat and eat.

Jess and the others went forward for their dishes. Gabe and young Jeb, having brought back a heap of chips for Jonathan, were given extra helpings. The coffee, having been packed along from their dawn camp and re-heated, was bitter as bile and as black as death, but they drank it without complaint, each busy with his private thoughts.

A rider approaching from the west hallooed the camp and they all dropped low to peer under the wagon at him. It was one of the immigrants riding alone. He was not one of those who had earlier come to the cow camp with old Eli Young. They let him ride in and dismount, walk around where they were eating, then Jonathan hospitably asked if he'd eaten. He hadn't, so Jonathan dished up a tin plate of their stew for him.

This immigrant was younger, perhaps no more than twenty, and he was built more like a Texan than a Yankee, tall and gangling lean, sun-darkened and smoke-eyed. He told them Eli Young had his party's share of mutual responsibility arranged for, and that, as soon as the sun failed, the immigrant patrols would start criss-crossing. He also said they'd sent out two scouts.

"Fellers who scouted durin' the war. Missourians," he told them, "who know their way around."

"Maybe up in Missouri they do," mumbled Potter Houston. "But this here is Comanche territory."

"Here, too," said the tall youth, turning to accept the plate and cup from Jonathan. "They were with the Army when it came down into Texas."

The Texans saw Potter's saber scar darken and his black gaze turned mean toward the settler. Before Potter got the chance, though, Jess looked him squarely in the eye and dropped his brows straight down in mute warning. Potter sat rigidly for a moment, then dropped his head and went to eating, his expression still darkly hostile, but tamed just enough by Jess's look to keep him quiet.

Hook-nosed, bronze-layered Harper Ellis, sitting with his back to the wagon wheel, his hat tipped far back, said: "Son, be better in Texas if you learned not to talk about the war." It was fatherly advice, and good advice, too. The immigrant blushed and concentrated on his plate of stew while an awkward silence ensued, broken eventually by Jess Howard's remark that with luck they'd be able to keep the renegades away.

The immigrant was a pale-haired, fresh-faced man, open and candid of expression. He wore a six-gun on his hip and packed a long-barreled rifle, but he looked out of place among those Texans.

Gabe went and got him a refill for his coffee cup, and gave him a white-toothed, jet black smile.

"It's a good country," Gabe softly said, " 'cept for maybe Comancheros and one or two other breeds of varmints. You folks'll find Texans right fine people . . . if you give 'em half a chance to be."

The youth returned Gabe's smile. "We heard all manner of tales. Some said Texans'd burn us out. Others said they wouldn't do any such a thing. The folks are sort of on edge. That's why we didn't stick to the main immigrant roads. Mister Young said it'd be better to just sort of go along mindin' our own business, causin' no trouble." The youth paused, looked straight at Potter, then said: "Be nice to have good neighbors again." It was almost an entreaty. Potter didn't say anything; he scarcely even looked up. But young Jeb, more nearly the immigrant youth's age than the others, spoke up.

"Hell, no finer folks on earth'n Texans. An' if there's fightin' tonight, you'll see we cut an' shoot with the best of 'em."

The immigrant grinned and Jeb grinned back. Jess Howard cocked an eye at the sky. Daylight was drawing to a close. There was a faintly acid scent to the air from curing grass, cooling rock, and lupine with its spiky blue flowers. He got up and strolled out a way to look southward. The land was totally, deceptively empty. Wayne Levitt walked out to him and commented on how peaceful it seemed. Instead of getting back a harmless answer, Jess turned and said: "Wayne, I don't give a damn what you did somewhere else, but don't walk away every time a settler comes around. We may need you."

Levitt's gray gaze whipped around and clung to Jess. He formed words behind his lips but in the end didn't offer them. He just bent down, plucked a grass blade, popped it between his teeth, and thoughtfully, silently chewed it.

Harper Ellis came out there, too, for a look at the empty plain. "Too bad we couldn't be another three days on the northward drive," he said. "Be out of Comanchero country by then." He gently nodded his head as though agreeing with himself, then squinted his eyes nearly closed and said: "Yonder, boys, yonder to the west a ways . . . dust."

They saw it, pale murkiness rising up against the smoky sky, far off near the drop-off of the empty horizon. Wayne said, coming from that southeasterly direction as it was, had to mean that the renegades had seen the circled-up wagon train and were making a leisurely scout over in that direction. "Hope them scouts those folks sent out don't happen to be down there. Too bad for them if they get caught south of the wagons and below the Comancheros."

Jess made an audible sigh. It was turning cool now, bland and fragrant like prairie evenings often are. The sky was red-streaked and darkly dull without a hint of wind. Sometimes it struck a man that when Nature was at her best, man was at his worst. "Well," he muttered, "let's get back and get rigged out."

Potter and Gabe were checking their weapons. Jonathan and the immigrant youth were softly, idly talking in the shade. When Jess returned, the others all looked at him. They had calm, hard faces, capable of killing without a qualm, or just as capable of laughing. Nature in the raw was seldom mild; these were natural men.

"Pair off," Jess said to them. "Gabe, you 'n' Wayne. Potter, you 'n' Harper. Jeb, you 'n' me."

"Hey," squawked Jonathan, hitching forward on his crippled legs. "I got to sit around again like the last time?"

Jess grinned with his lips but not with his eyes. "If anything happens to you, Jonathan, who'll cook and rustle firewood an' hitch the team an' . . . ?"

"Be damned," snarled the older man fiercely, hopping up and down in anger. "No matter how dark it gets this here white canvas top's goin' to stick out like a snowbank for them renegades to zero in on. Now I went along with it last time, but, by God, Jess, you got no right to make me do it again."

Jess's little mirthless grin faded. He stood staring at the *cocinero*. Jonathan was a good man, crippled and sometimes cranky, but all the same a good man. "Do what you like," he said. "I was thinkin' someone's got to watch our wagon is all. If they get up this close, they'll fire it to see to shoot by."

A hastening rider coming on sounded out there upon the gloomy plain westerly. The immigrant youth started on a run to the other side of the wagon. Potter caught his arm and wrenched him back with a snarl.

"You want to get killed?" he demanded. "Let him get up into sight, boy, don't *ever* rush out like that. See *him* before he sees *you*." As he released the immigrant's arm, he grumbled: "Wonder to me the Yanks ever won the war a-tall."

A quick, soft call came down through the gloom to them and every man stiffened where he stood. It wasn't a man's voice making that call; it was a woman's voice! Even Jess was frozen to the ground with astonishment. Only the immigrant moved forward. "My sister," he said.

They all hurried around to the far side of the wagon. The girl who rode up was astride a big, powerful black horse, sleek and shiny even in the dusk. She wore a rusty-colored split riding skirt and a pale blouse. Her mane of heavy taffy hair was held back by a small ribbon and she had a rifle across her lap.

The men crowded hungrily forward. They'd known there would be womenfolk with the immigrant wagons, and it had been a long month since they'd even seen a woman, but this wasn't just a woman, this was a girl in her late teens or early twenties as beautiful to look upon as anything any of them had ever seen. Even bitter-eyed, stalwart Potter Houston swept off his hat and looked straight up at her without any hint of his usual hardness apparent.

"John," she said to the immigrant youth. "Get your horse. You're supposed to be with the others. We're making up a party."

Jess moved in closer to her. "A party?" he inquired.

She looked down at him, her face alive with urgency. "We had two scouts out," she said. "One came back nearly dead and only the horse of the other one returned . . . with blood over the saddle. Mister Young is making up a party to go after him, in case he's hurt and not dead."

"No," breathed Jess. "You das'n't do that. It's a deliberate trap to get your menfolk away from the wagons."

She never batted an eye as she said to Jess: "Then it's going to succeed, mister. We're from Missouri. If you think only Texans know how to fight, saddle up and come along. We'll soon show you differently."

Potter and Harper went closer, too, as her brother ran for his mount. Potter said: "Lady, Jess is plumb right. You strip those wagons of armed men and break the agreement you folks have with us to patrol, and you'll be layin' us all wide open for attack."

She swung away from Jess to consider swarthy, saber-scarred Potter Houston. Their eyes met and held as she said: "If you have objections, ride back with me and tell them to Mister Young. He's our wagon master and he knows what's best."

"Not this time," said Potter. "You wait. I'll fetch a horse."

As Potter swung, Jess caught his arm; he told Potter to fetch back two horses.

The immigrant youth rode up, astride his animal. The girl looked impatiently after Potter, who trotted back where their mounts were. She clearly regretted having to wait. Gabe and Wayne Levitt moved off a little way and fell to talking. Gabe gestured southeastward with an outflung arm. Wayne listened and slowly nodded. The pair of them went over to Jess and said they thought, as long as the immigrants weren't going to wait, that the Texans should look to their own protection, and the best way to do that would be for two of them to go downcountry and lie out there on the ground to give warning with gunshots the moment they spotted enemies.

Jess vetoed this idea and ordered them all to remain at the wagon until he got back from the immigrant camp. At that moment Potter came back riding one horse and leading another. He tossed the free reins to Jess, who stepped up. As a parting warning Jess said: "Stay right here and don't go wandering around, any of you. We'll get back as quick as we can."

He and the two immigrants wheeled and went

loping eastward. The handsome girl's black horse was as strong as he was big; he led them all the way back across the intervening distance at a powerful lope, and, although the Texas horses were just as stout, they couldn't quite keep up with him.

Jess rode easily in the saddle, watching the girl. She rode as well as any man, handled that big stout horse like he was a pony, and her taffy-colored hair fell in cascading waves across her shoulders. It was easy to see the resemblance between the immigrant youth and his sister, but if the boy had iron in his constitution, he hadn't shown it. The girl had, though, and she continued to show it right up to the moment they slackened speed within sight of the circled wagons where a man loped out on a bay horse to intercept and challenge them. It was that same burly, powerful man who had been riding earlier with old Eli Young. He passed them on and rode back to his sentry post.

They rode into the wagon circle where men were saddling horses and running back and forth for their weapons. Eli was standing where a party of riflemen was grouped, talking. When he recognized Jess and Potter, he shouldered past and headed for them.

The wagon camp was alive with activity. From within one of the wagons a woman's anguished wails rose and fell. There wasn't a smiling face anywhere around as the Texans dismounted in front of old Eli Young.

VI

Eli listened to Jess's protests and afterward turned adamant. He told them he knew what their earlier agreement had been. He also said he realized it might be a trap by the renegades to draw his men away from the wagons. But he also said that, if they got one good look at the Comancheros, he and his men, they would never get any closer to the wagons than that.

Jess grew exasperated. "You don't understand how these renegades fight, Mister Young. They aren't goin' to charge you like a troop of cavalry. They'll split up, half to draw you off and engage you, half to sneak up here and stampede my cattle or attack your train. I realize how you feel . . . you've lost one good man and maybe another one's dead down there somewhere. But avenging them isn't going to be easy, and, if this thing is the trap we believe it to be, you aren't going to do anything but leave your womenfolk in deadly peril."

A bull-like younger man strode up, gazed at Eli, and nodded, then strode away again. The old man said: "Mister Howard, you're welcome to ride along if you like." He then strode away after the bull-like Missourian who'd just given him some kind of a signal.

Potter turned slowly to follow Young's progress, his swarthy face getting black as thunder. "The

96

damned fool!" he exclaimed. "The damned fool Yankee."

Jess saw the handsome girl approaching and growled under his breath. Potter turned and fell silent until she came up to them, then he mentioned her name and said in a toned-down way what he thought: "Miss Wheelock, what you folks are doin' doesn't make good sense. Someone of you had better hammer some logic into old Eli's skull before he gets you women massacred and the men cut off out there by Comancheros."

"Did you try?" she sweetly asked.

"Yes'm, I tried."

"Then, Mister Houston, you must know we're not a people who're easily influenced." She switched her attention briefly to Jess, but it was obvious her interest was in Potter. To Jess she said: "You can stand here all night, Mister Howard." Her bittersweet tone of voice inferred that if Jess had any manhood to him at all he'd ride with the others.

Jess did not reply. Over her rounded shoulder he saw mounted men forming farther back inside the wagon circle. They bristled with armament. Old Eli, his chin whiskers in the wild night more than ever like something out of Biblical times, brandished his rifle for silence, then thundered at his men: "You saw what the fiends did to Ezra, and somewhere out there they've left Jubal a-lyin'. Well now, we've always said we'd go to Texas to settle and farm the soil and live at peace with others, but that if we got pushed, we'd push back twice as hard. I look on this as our first challenge, so we'd best scourge the enemy so the word'll spread an' others'll leave us be. How say you, men?"

They gave a loud cheer for old Eli. Potter, standing back with his hat in both hands and distant lamp glow making that saber scar look evil, shook his head. "He's crazy," Potter muttered, low and soft. "Jess, he's sacrificin' these folks like sheep. Someone ought to stop him."

The beautiful girl was still there. She heard and said: "Would you like to try, Mister Houston?" And smiled up into his eyes with very clear meaning. Everyone inside that wagon circle, even the girls and young boys, was armed with a carbine, a rifle, or a pistol. Potter said nothing.

Eli led his men out between two wagons. They were over twenty strong and very capable-looking although in a land of belt guns and carbines, their pistols pushed into waistbands and their long-barreled rifles looked a little odd. Still, it was not difficult to see that those dirt-farming Missourians were not novices at riding out to fight, nor that old Eli was an adequate leader for them.

Jess stepped over to a wagon tongue between two wagons and sat down upon it, looking around. There were women and girls and boys and old men inside the circle. As Potter had said, old Eli in his fire and brimstone zeal had left these people not only unprepared, but leaderless. A little girl with a tipped-up nose and freckles went past, looked up at Jess Howard, and threw him a wicked little girl smile. With a flick of her pigtails she was gone. He raised his eyes to Peggy Wheelock. She looked straight back. He said: "Potter, go on back. Fetch the boys back here. Help Jonathan hitch the team and drive the wagon on over."

"What about the herd, Jess?"

"Well," said Jess, standing up and gazing at Potter. "What would your decision be? We can't salvage both, not just seven of us."

Potter nodded and put his hat on. "Sure," he murmured, "be back directly." He strode back out where they'd left their horses.

The girl kept studying Jess. She eventually said: "You think there's too much light inside the circle." It was a statement, not a question. He nodded up at her.

"They use your own light against you when they sneak up low on the ground, Miss Peggy. Sometimes they use arrows instead of guns because they're silent and you can't tell where they're shooting from. You got to have someone with a gun under every wagon, otherwise they'll breach your circle. Once inside, they fire wagon canvas to see to shoot you by. They don't fight like soldiers at all, Miss Peggy. They fight to kill and plunder."

"All right," she said crisply. "I'll go tell the others."

He nodded at her. "You're awfully handsome to be bossin' a fightin' crew, Miss Peggy. Maybe I'd better do it."

Her eyes softened the faintest bit toward him. "Then I'll go along and tell them you're in charge," she said. "As for the other, I'd like to ask you a question."

"Fire away, Miss Peggy. What question?"

"Is . . . does Potter Houston have a wife down in Texas?"

Jess's eye widened. "A wife . . . Potter? No, Potter has no wife."

"And that knife scar . . . ?"

"Yankee saber at Sabine Pass during the war. Potter doesn't much care for Yankees."

"Is he an honest, truthful man, Mister Howard?"

"Yes'm, and he's a good man, but he's got bad memories inside him that sometimes make him bitter about things."

"Could a woman change that in him, Mister Howard?"

Jess softly smiled at her. She was one of the finest-looking women he'd ever seen and he'd been up the trail a time or two. "*A* woman could, Miss Peggy, I'd bet money on that, but not just *any* woman. She'd have to be . . . well . . . all woman, Miss Peggy."

"Thank you, Mister Howard," she said, and half

turned from him. "Now let's go tell the others what has to be done."

Jess walked out into the noise and turmoil of the wagon camp. That little freckled child with the tipped-up nose stood back with several other children and her parents smiling her hero worship at him as he went past. He paused to give one pigtail a gentle pull, then strode on with Peggy Wheelock to where seven or eight old men were charging extra muskets atop a rickety old table, surrounded by half-grown youths and women.

He wasted no time; his talk was crisp and matter-of-fact. It was in the back of his mind that perhaps, with luck, these people just might be able to keep the Comancheros engaged and they might not then hit his herd, which was scattered northeastward in its search for better graze and water. But it seemed unlikely anything as skittish as his longhorn cattle wouldn't stampede in wild panic when the gunfire erupted, because if thunder could do it, then so could a fierce gun battle. He anticipated nothing less at this place. Well, the cattle would probably run northward, which was the general direction of Kansas anyway, but beyond that he couldn't speculate. He could only stay where he was, supervise the defense, and trust in whatever Divine Providence interested in getting Texas beef up north into Yankee railroad pens did to lend a hand.

Surprisingly the immigrants still had plenty of arms and ammunition even after Eli's party had pulled out. Equally as surprising, the women handled guns almost as well as the boys and men. When he'd told them how they must put boxes and blanket rolls and tick mattresses in front of them beneath the wagons, douse all but four lanterns, and detail loaders to keep their guns charged, they told him all those dispositions had already been made. When he put most of the men southward from which direction he expected the renegades to attack, Peggy Wheelock told him that old Eli had already said the same thing.

He considered the mob of women and older men, youths and stalwart girls. "Someone ought to stay inside one of the stoutest wagons with the little children," he said. Two women with pistols belted to their middles stepped forth to say that was their chore. "Then," he said, "everyone to his . . . or her . . . position, an', if you see anything moving out beyond the wagon circle, challenge once, then fire. Shoot low. They'll be belly crawling more'n likely. Just one more thing. My wagon's on its way over here with my drovers. They'll sing out, so don't shoot at them."

Peggy stood with him as the people moved off. She saw his expression and said: "Don't fret, Mister Howard. Eli held musket trials once a week. We can shoot."

He slumped against a water cask. "If you'd told me you folks were this well organized, it'd have save me a couple of gray hairs, Miss Peggy."

"You didn't ask me, Mister Howard. You just assumed, since we weren't native-born Texans, that we were helpless. Someday you should travel up through Missouri. Our men were with General Taylor and General Scott in Mexico. We've been pushing back the frontier for as long as you folks have been pushing back Comanches."

He grinned at her. "I reckon I ought to make the trip at that. Tell me, Miss Peggy. They got any more like you up there?"

Someone sang out that a wagon was coming in from the east. Moments later a shrill Rebel yell split the darkness with its chilling echo and Jess crossed the wagon circle at a trot to lend a hand at pushing back barricades so old Jonathan could tool their camp rig inside the circle while Harper and Gabe, Jeb and Wayne Levitt drove in their saddle animals.

Potter swung off and turned to unsaddling. The others also moved efficiently to do what must be done. Old Jonathan and an immigrant who was even older yanked off chain harness and flung it over the forewheels of the wagon so the team animals were loose. Jess didn't have to tell his men what to do; they'd been in this identical situation before. If not exactly, then at least close enough to know without asking what was required of them.

When they were finished off-saddling, they congregated around Jess. He told them how well prepared the settlers were and old Jonathan didn't believe it, so he went poking around the circle, peering under each wagon and between them, where box barricades stood manned. Potter drifted off by himself. So did Wayne Levitt. Gabe and Jeb offered to scout out a way on foot, and Jess let them go without any warnings. They didn't need to be remonstrated with.

Jess turned when someone spoke his name in a piping tone. The little pigtailed young lady was there with a tin cup of black coffee and her dazzling smile. He dropped to one knee to sip coffee and tell her she should be in the wagon with the other children. She agreed without a murmur, turned, and marched off.

Gradually, except for loose livestock inside the wagon circle, the camp turned dark and quiet. Now and then when strange horses met, they squealed, but aside from that there was only a little furtive movement here and there and low talk. Wayne Levitt approached Jess with his carbine hooked in the crook of an arm. "Would you say," he quietly asked, "this was a lousy place for a man to find himself a woman?"

Jess guessed what he meant and said: "No, not exactly. But I'd sure say there must be better times an' places for it, Wayne."

"Yeah. I reckon that's how I should've said it. Anyway, it 'pears to me if he looked for ten years and a thousand miles he couldn't have found one as near fit to put a ring in his nose. An' fine-lookin' in the bargain. About the finest set-up woman I ever saw."

Jess agreed. Peggy Wheelock was something a man could look at once and never again forget. "Got spirit, too," Jess murmured. "Wayne, you reckon you an' I'll ever be that lucky?"

"Naw," muttered Levitt with a hard wag of his head. "You know a damned sight better'n that. Some men just aren't meant to get good women. Besides, how many *good* women are there in this world? I'll tell you, Jess. Damned precious few. I'm tellin' you this from experience. Damned precious few." Levitt grounded his gun and fished around for a tobacco sack. As he went to work making a smoke, he bitterly shook his head.

Someone southward beyond the wagon circle made the cry of a mourning dove. At once Jess turned and walked briskly away.

It was black Gabe and young Jeb. When they clambered inside the circle, Gabe rolled his eyes and said the most dangerous part had been convincing the immigrants they weren't enemies.

"What'd you find?" Jess demanded.

"Skulkers a-comin'," Gabe replied. "And a long way off we heard a fight goin' on. Sounded like the settlers done run into the other bunch of 'em. Big fight, too. Lots of gunfire. Didn't sound to me like those immigrants got ambushed, sounded more like they found the other band of

Comancheros an' made a run on 'em. Lots of noise and gunshots, but a long way southward."

Jess nodded his head.

"Nothin' we can do 'bout that," added Gabe, looking back over his shoulder. "But the skulkers aren't more'n a mile off, comin' up on foot. Couldn't tell how many, but enough of 'em an' they's scattered out from west to east."

Jess said: "Go along the line and pass the word. Then take positions southward. I'll meet you down there after I've also passed the word. Good luck."

"Yeah," muttered Gabriel. "The same to you, Mistah Jess."

As word spread that they'd soon be under attack, the silence deepened and lingered. Even the loose animals inside the circle seemed to sense impending trouble; they milled around uneasily. Four lanterns burned; all else was in darkness. The wait was worse than the fighting.

VII

It was a long wait, too. Those renegades out there knew all the tricks of night fighting; how to use light against the attacked; how to belly crawl where the grass was tallest right up to within ten feet of a defender; how to kill without a sound. Even how to imitate the voices of their enemies to divert attention. But this time they had seven seasoned Texans to cope with who knew all the

Comanchero tricks, so when old Jonathan, hatless and kneeling with his carbine snugged back, saw a pale wraith rise up fifty feet off and strain with his bow arm, Jonathan fired. That was the first shot; it was also the first fatality for the renegade's arrow went high into the air as impact and a smashed breastbone drove the man over backward in a wild moment of threshing.

Jess and Jeb were at a boxed-in barricade between two of the southward wagons. They saw that killing. They also saw the lancing red wink of muzzle blast here and there from beneath the nearest wagons where women and immigrant old men opened up with a ground-sluicing fire that snapped off grass stalks six inches above the ground.

"They'll do, by God!" the youth exclaimed. "Never seen womenfolk under fire before, have you, Jess?"

Jess didn't reply. A long ripple of gunfire erupted from west to east out where the renegades were prone and scattered. They, too, were firing low. Because the moonlight was so poor, all Jess could fire at was the abrupt flash of orange flame far out. It was not a very reliable target, for once the Comancheros and their bronco Comanches fired, they all hit the dirt and rolled clear.

But one thing became immediately apparent to attacked as well as attackers—this was going to be no easy victory for the besiegers. After a while their gunfire slackened and a chilling lull ensued.

To Jess this meant they'd tried the southward wagons, found them too well defended, and were now congregating out there in the shadowy night to decide which way, left or right, they'd move now to hit the circle again.

He sent Jeb around to pass the word along both sides: prepare to be attacked next. Shoot at anything that moved outside the circle. Be very alert. Cry out for help if a rush was made upon any particular wagon. Then Jess strained to detect sound out there where the attackers were. There wasn't so much as the drag of a rifle barrel over stone, not even a cough or the tinkle of a spur.

A thick-set youth with a struggling, downy moustache walked over and said he'd had to shoot a horse, that an arrow had come from somewhere and pierced it through the gullet. Jess asked about other casualties. The youth shook his head. There were no others. Jess sent him back to his post and strolled over where Jonathan and the old immigrant who'd helped crippled Jonathan pull harness off the Texas team squatted, muttering back and forth, and kept a squinty-eyed vigil. Jonathan looked, and made a wolfish smile. "We got one," he said. "I reckon that'll learn the varmints. They weren't expectin' us to be ready."

"Keep watch," Jess said, and walked on. Wayne Levitt backed out from beneath a wagon and hung there on hands and knees, looking up as Jess came along. He spat and shook his head.

"They'll hit the east side," said Wayne, and had scarcely gotten the words out than a great scream rose up out in the yonder dark, and shadows rose up off the ground in a wild rush. It was a massacre. Guns roared and flashed all along the wagon circle from beneath, from behind the interspersed barricades, even over the sides of the rigs where immigrants crouched low with only their gun barrels exposed under the soiled canvas tops.

Jess sprang to an opening and joined in. A fire arrow hit canvas but it had too much momentum; it passed straight on through and fell to the ground where someone stamped it out. The frightful screams stopped. Attackers dropped flat to escape the hail of lead, fired and rolled and fired again. A wiry shadow gave a shriek, sprang up out of the grass, and hurled itself forward and low, sliding in under a wagon. Jess dropped, swung around, and threw himself under the same wagon. He was too late. Wayne Levitt was already there. The renegade and Levitt met head-on. There was a little wisp of a woman under the same wagon. Wayne managed to grasp the renegade's knife-holding hand at the wrist and roll to heave the Comanche off balance. At the same time the little woman pushed a foot-long Dragoon pistol against the Indian's ribs and pulled the trigger. The explosion was muffled but the impact wrenched the man free from Wayne Levitt's grim hold. He rolled back out from under the wagon and flopped over onto his back, dead.

Jess looked at the woman. She put a hand up to her lips and lowered the pistol to the ground. She stared hard at her victim, then quickly flung around, crawled from beneath the wagon, and ran. Wayne picked up her pistol and peered backward where she was hanging onto the corner of a wagon, bent far over. "You go right ahead an' heave," he said, although she was too distant to hear him. "You're bigger'n a lot of men I've known."

Jess peered out where the red flashes were continuing. "Get back to it," he said to Wayne. "You can thank her later."

Several more fire arrows came over but only one hung up in the canvas of a wagon, and someone inside reached up, tore the thing loose, and heaved water on the little flame. More of that chilling screaming began. It was harmless except to the nerves of women and children, and as long as everyone on the east side was engaged in a desperate fight for life, it didn't even have much effect on them.

Several immigrant men left their positions across the circle to give aid. Jess angrily yelled for them to get back where they belonged. Far away over the sporadic gunfire he heard horsemen loping up. It could be more Comancheros, perhaps survivors from the fight with the immigrants under old Eli Young, or it could be some of the attackers getting ready to try a charge into the wagon circle. He yelled out at the top of his voice for everyone

110

to look sharp, to be ready for a mounted attack.

But it never came. Whatever those horsemen were up to out in the dark, they did not make a run on the wagons, and, as before, the gunfire began to dwindle again. First, the lower end of the circle had been hit, then the easterly wagons. Now it was the turn of those to the west across the circle or perhaps up front, to the north. It didn't occur to Jess that those mounted men weren't going to charge the wagons. He had no time to speculate until Potter and Harper came walking briskly along to where he stood re-loading.

Harper said: "Jess, did you hear those riders out a ways?"

Jess said he'd heard them: "What of it?

"They rode north!" exclaimed Harper, and bit the last word off with hard emphasis. "North. Up where the longhorns arc."

Harper's meaning was very clear. Comanchero horsemen heading up where the herd was meant they were going to attempt one of two things: either run off a big bunch of the cattle, or try and turn a segment of the herd, head it straight for the forted-up wagons, then howl and shoot their guns behind it to stampede the critters straight into the defensive circle.

Potter turned and looked down as Wayne Levitt crawled from beneath his wagon and stood up to join them. Potter said: "Jess, fire'll turn 'em if they run 'em over us. But gunfire sure as hell won't. It might stack up a lot of dead ones but it sure as hell won't stop the rest from bowlin' over the wagons and stampeding into this camp."

"Fire!" exclaimed Wayne, looking at Potter. "You crazy? Those damned renegades out there could pick us off like flies on a wall if we lit a big enough fire to turn a stampede."

"Take your choice," snapped Potter. "Get shot at or ground into jelly by maybe four, five hundred crazed longhorns."

"Maybe them fellers didn't go after cattle," said Wayne. "Maybe they just circled around to hit the wagons across the circle."

Jess shook his head at that. If the renegades had had such a plan in mind, by now they'd have been on the opposite side, attacking. He looked at Potter and Harper Ellis. It was his decision and his alone; the immigrants wouldn't understand, and he had no time to explain it to all of them. One thing was certain. As Wayne Levitt had said, a bonfire large enough to spook the longhorns and turn them away from the wagon circle would light up the inside of their defensive circle as bright as day. They would be pitilessly limned while their enemies would be out there, hidden in the darkness, able to pick them off left and right.

He said a savage oath. "Potter, you 'n' Harper start gathering whatever these folks have that'll burn. Crawl out under the northward wagons and push that stuff out as far from the circle as you can

112

safely get it. Don't fire it until you hear the herd coming or until I tell you to. Pour coal oil over it so it'll go up fast if you have to light it."

"Then pray," mumbled Wayne Levitt. "Because we're all as good as dead the second you light up." He dropped down and crawled back under his wagon because, out yonder, the gunfire had turned brisk again.

Potter and Harper walked back up the line of wagons. Jess stepped in close to a barricade manned by three youths in their teens and tried his hardest to discern the sound of mounted men again. He failed. Either those riders had gone too far upcountry to be detected, or they'd dismounted out there somewhere. He did not, in his secret thoughts, believe the latter at all.

A Comanche was making a death chant somewhere out in the night, his voice rising and falling, rising and falling. Either someone close to him had been shot, or else he was chanting hopefully for the death of the immigrants inside their defensive circle. Jess didn't know which and didn't particularly care which.

Black Gabriel came along with a canteen slung over one shoulder, his carbine in the other hand. As Jess turned, Gabe said: "Got a man hit under one of them wagons. Fetchin' him some water." Gabe shook his head. "Bad, bad," he muttered, and paced along southward.

It was dangerous now to try and cross the circle

unless one darted swiftly because the livestock had smelled blood and rushed around kicking up dust, squealing and kicking at anything close. Whenever people had to move, they did so by staying as close to the wagons as possible. There was some danger, also, to the people manning the barricades between wagons; occasionally a bullet-stung horse would run blindly around.

But gradually the attackers slackened their gun-fire again. These lulls came often. They were invariably more prolonged than the episodes of furious firing, but at least when the Comancheros were attacking, Jess could figure out where they were and about what they were up to. In the silence he couldn't even accurately guess what they were doing.

It was during the lull that three women, one of them Peggy Wheelock, came down the line with a big granite-ware coffee pot and some tin cups. Peggy filled a cup and passed it to Jess, who thanked her. After the first gulp, he made a face; they had laced the coffee liberally with raw whiskey.

"It helps with the pain if you're hit," Peggy said to him, very solemn. "Potter told me what he and Mister Ellis have to do out beyond the north-ward wagons. I want you to know I understand, Jess."

He handed back the empty cup with a very pleasant warmth fanning out through his body. It had been several hours since he'd eaten. "I'm glad you understand," he said. "I hope your friends do."

"They will," said the lovely girl, and moved along with her two female companions to offer drinks of that fiery coffee to the other defenders.

Jess looked after them until a gangling youth stood up behind him and gingerly flexed one leg. He had a broken case of cartridges on the ground where he'd been kneeling and a hole through the tall crown of his hat through which he soberly poked a finger as he said: "One time I heard a feller say up in the Chagrin Creek country that once a feller's come close to bein' kilt, he don't scare real easy afterward." He raised his clear blue gaze and shook his head. " 'Tain't so, mister. That's how close I come, an' I'm plumb scairt t' death."

Jess smiled at the boy. "Me, too, pardner, me, too. But bein' scairt and turnin' tail are two different things. Now you squat back down there and load up. The fight's not over yet by a far sighting."

That puny little sickle moon was floating serenely up there in its purple pasture with speckled stars all around it, giving less light than a herd of Texas fireflies would give. The night was warm and otherwise balmy. Jess guessed it to be close to 10:00. He wondered how that fight had come out down south. There would be casualties among Eli's riders even if they'd triumphed. Texas, as the saying went, was a hard land on woman and mules. On widows trying to scratch a livelihood from the bitterbrush prairies or the plum thicket bottoms along the creek and rivers, it could be a merciless place.

But life was an insoluble mystery; whatever happened this night might change forever a number of human lives and destinies, but wondering about it wouldn't soften a single blow.

He turned to gaze out beyond the wagons where that ghostly silence ran on. Maybe, with luck, they could cut down enough renegades at least to make it possible so that the next batch of settlers and drovers wouldn't have to sacrifice their folks like this. Maybe that was the purpose of every fight, to make the world a safer place. He longed for a smoke but didn't trouble to make one. The trouble with that kind of logic, he told himself, was simply that as soon as one band of killers was vanquished, invariably another band appeared to take their place. Life was a process of struggle and strife, killing or dying, and whether men wished for it to be that way or not, that's how it was. Kill or be killed. It always had been that way. It always would be that way. It was enough to sicken a man, sometimes.

He decided to make that smoke, after all.

VIII

Jonathan hallooed from down among the southerly wagons. Jess went down there; Jonathan wouldn't have made that yell if it hadn't been important.

He didn't quite get to the *cocinero*'s barricade before he heard the drum roll of oncoming horsemen. Others also heard it as the seconds ticked off. This could not be the same bunch of riders Jess had heard earlier for two reasons. The first was they were rushing up from the wrong direction; those other horsemen had loped off northward. The second reason was simply because there were too many of them.

He ran on down where Jonathan had his carbine resting across a barrel, tracking the sound of those approaching riders. He rested one hand lightly upon the older man's shoulder.

"Easy," he murmured. "Easy, Jonathan. If the Lord's with us tonight, it won't be more Comancheros."

Suddenly those riders halted beyond gun range. For twenty seconds there wasn't a sound, then someone far off to the southeast, down through the black night, fired a gun. At once a man's throaty roar of defiance rang out; all those riders wheeled and went pell-mell in the direction of that solitary shot. Seconds later gunfire erupted, wild and thunderous. Those were Eli's men returning!

The immigrants raised a howl of exultation and relief. Even Jess and Jonathan sang out encouragement as the mounted Missourians charged into the stepped-up gunfire of the surprised Comancheros out beyond the wagon circle. It was, for those renegades, an unfortunate time for them to be hit by enemies; a goodly portion of their crew had gone north after the cattle. Those who were still out there on foot didn't number very many. After the howling Missourians rode over them, shooting right and left, they numbered considerably less.

Men were screaming to one another. It was impossible to determine the cry of renegades from the wrathful howls of their attackers. Jess had to run forward and block a barricade that had been removed, to prevent some of the immigrants from rushing forth to join in that yonder battle.

"Get back!" he roared at the people. "In the dark an' on foot out there, your own men would shoot you down. Get back!"

Wayne Levitt came up to help. So did Gabe and young Jeb. They maintained order but only by hurling their bodies against thrusting Missourians of both sexes.

Potter and Harper Ellis came running. Potter was calling for Jess and the other Texans to saddle up. Finally some of that bedlam out there in the darkness diminished; the straining people inside their wagon circle shuffled back a little way, breathlessly waiting. That was when Jess ran to saddle up. His men were already doing the same thing. As they scrambled up over leather and called out with gestures for the people to stand clear of the open place between two wagons, Jess told them to stand watch. He said the battle was not yet over and the renegades could still get inside. Then he led his men out beyond the wagons, swung and called to some of the Missourians to close the breach again.

Ten feet from the wagons they came upon a dead Comanche. A hundred feet beyond they saw a dead Comanchero, the top of his head blown off. The fight out there had swirled westerly a mile. Guns were loud out there but their muzzle blasts were scarcely more than pinpricks of dazzling light in the distance. Somewhere, southward, a man went racing away on a straining horse. It wouldn't be a Missourian, so they opened fire without anything more than sound to aim by, then they hastened onward until the flashes of orange were close enough to make them cease their headlong run.

But the fight was nearly over by that time. Horsemen loomed up and somewhere a man was yelling for quarter. A second man joined him. Suddenly it all ended. One moment there was gunfire, the next moment there was none, just the keening whine of an injured Comanchero and the husky croak of two surrendering renegades.

Jess's Texans identified themselves to Eli's men. The two parties came together out there, on foot, and at once the question was breathlessly asked:

"How fared the wagon circle?" The Texans assured everyone with old Eli the wagon circle had not been breached, and, although they could not say there had been no casualties, they *could* say few had been hit. Then a Missourian distracted them all by calling forth that he had two prisoners. They all silently paced over and halted, their horses behind them, their rifles in hand, to stare.

One of the renegades was a Mexican, or some kind of a half- or quarter-breed. The other one was a blue-eyed, tall, stalwart American. The American gazed around with the settled expression of dull expectancy across his whisker-stubbled face, but the 'breed stared glibly, explaining how he'd been forced to ride with the other renegades at peril for his life. He even smiled and gestured with his hands to indicate how amiable he genuinely was, until Eli Young lazily raised a bony hand and struck him hard across the mouth.

"Shut your mouth," old Eli said. "We lost two good men tonight, and three hurt, by the likes of you."

Potter Houston bent his head and whispered something to Jess, who nodded and moved up closer to speak to old Eli. "Mister Young, we can't waste time. Half the band that hit your wagons rode northward not long ago to turn the longhorns and stampede them against the circle."

Old Eli turned quickly. "Then let's get up there," he said, and reached for the saddle horn. As he settled into his saddle with a solid tiredness to the movement, he looked around, fastened his eyes upon that burly, powerful man he'd had with him at the initial meeting between immigrants and Texans, nodded without a word, then led the others northward in a long lope.

Jess was riding beside Gabe, with Harper Ellis on the off side, a thousand yards upcountry, when the two unmistakable gunshots rang out far back. Not a one of the Missourians even so much as glanced back. Up ahead in the lead, old Eli's thatch of bristly, grizzled hair stood like spikes in the night air, his splayed-out big beard strongly lifted and pointing the way ahead.

They made a solid rumble, speeding along through the black hush. Once or twice cattle sprang out of their beds and went flinging away, out of their onward course. Eli slowly twisted to look for Jess. "Which way?" he asked.

Jess had no idea; there wasn't a sound up here. "Split up," he said on the spur of the moment. "You lead your crew to the west and north, then after a mile or so swing eastward. I'll take my men westerly, then up north and around until we meet."

Eli nodded, then he said: "But you'll need some of my men, won't you?"

Potter Houston drawled: "Naw. There's six Texans here and only one fight. We already got 'em outnumbered."

White teeth shone in dark faces on both sides; Eli

121

lifted his rein hand; Jess did likewise; the two parties wheeled away from one another and loped away. They began encountering cattle almost immediately. Not bedded cattle but critters standing up, alert and wide-eyed.

Gabe said, after a mile had been covered without any sign of Comancheros: "They up north by now, Mistah Jess. You can see by the way the critters is standin' that they done smelled men just a short while ago."

Potter and young Jeb agreed. Harper Ellis suggested they cut short their easterly ride and swing due north. That's what they did, and at once encountered a dense mass of cattle that they dared not break into or they'd start the stampede instead of the Comancheros starting it.

But when Jess veered off, leading them out and around that writhing sea of razorbacks and *clicking*, ghostly horns in the dark, he did so for another reason, also. If they happened to be in the middle of the longhorns when the renegades somewhere northward opened up with gunfire, stampeding cattle would charge southward right over the top of the Texans.

They finally found a way through and booted their animals over into a lope again, northward. That was when they heard the first gunshot. But it wasn't northward; it was westward *and* northward.

"Now what in the hell?" Potter called out perplexedly.

If the Comancheros were starting the stampede, they were far off course to the west; they should have been due northward. "Maybe," sang out Harper, also puzzled, "them immigrants come onto 'em before they could get into position."

Jess swerved when several more irregularly spaced, ragged gunshots sounded. The cattle they passed were jumping frantically to their feet. Whoever was doing that shooting, they were on the verge of starting the cattle off. Suddenly there was a great deal of gunfire, but farther westward. It didn't make a whole lot of sense to the Texans but they headed in the direction of the firming-up fight.

As before, when they got close enough to see pinpricks of gun flame, they slowed. The cattle over to the west were loosely trotting northward and castward, away from the battle scene, but that fight out there was going farther and farther westward. It looked to the Texas men as though Eli's Missourians had stumbled onto the Comancheros and were now being chased off by them.

"A feint," Jess finally pronounced, when he saw a series of moving, mounted men turn and fire to the rear. "Hell, old Eli's using his *cabeza*. He's feintin' them into chasin' him *away* from the herd."

The Texans loped along, swinging southward now, until they were parallel with the exultant Comancheros, then, as they turned northward, Potter Houston let off his chilling Rebel yell. They set their horses straight toward the Comancheros and opened with carbines and handguns from a distance of two hundred yards. They closed fast. It was a wild, rather foolhardy thing to do because the Missourians, off on their left, were still firing, but no one ever accused fighting Texans of being cautious in battle.

The Comancheros were caught unexpectedly by the Rebel yell and the wild gunfire. They hauled back in bewilderment. It only took a wild moment for Jess's crew to get into range with their hail of continuing lead. Then the renegades fought their frightened mounts around to flee. At once the Missourians reversed and also charged. After that the fight became a series of individual little deadly duels between Comancheros straining every sinew to break away and escape, and their grim enemies who rode them down left and right.

When it ultimately ended, there were dead men and horses scattered across two miles of the northward country. Potter Houston had one captive. He'd roped the man off his horse to drag him to death, but when the last shot was fired, Jess cut in front of Potter inadvertently, causing Houston to halt. Seconds later the others also came up.

Old Eli gazed stonily at the prisoner. He was an Indian, short, massively broad, and as brown as a Texas cutbank. "Shoot him," Eli said bitterly. "The filthy whelp." Ten guns swung to bear. The Comanche bared his teeth; like all the warriors of his race he did not fear death in the least. They shot him, and, since two slugs broke strands in Potter's lariat, he didn't bother retrieving it, but cast off the dally and flung the end of the rope down beside the dead man.

"We better look for wounded ones," someone said among the Missourians. "It's the Christian thing to do . . . put 'em out of their misery."

"Go right ahead," stated swarthy Potter Houston. "Me, I'm headin' back for the wagons."

Most of them turned and started back. There were four Missourians with wounds. Eli explained to Jess that they'd found their missing scout, shot and scalped. He also said, after that, when they also came upon the Comancheros lying in the grass to ambush the Missourians, he couldn't restrain his men.

"They killed 'em all, but for a couple who ran away. Seventeen by my count, Mister Howard."

Jess was impressed by the fighting prowess of these immigrants from the north. So were his men. Gabe rolled his eyes around and Wayne Levitt nodded back at him. Yankees these men might be, but hardier battlers did not exist in Texas. They'd get along in the Lone Star State.

Eli went on speaking. "We lost two other men in that skirmish down there." He twisted left and right in his saddle as though to count noses. "A few punctures," he added, not asking if his men had acquired any fresh injuries during the recent fight, evidently because, seeing them all riding upright in their saddles, he didn't believe they could be seriously hurt. "But we've come through, and we've taught our enemies we're not to be pushed."

"You have done that," drawled Harper Ellis, nodding at the old man. "Yes, sir, Mister Young, you've done that right smart."

They heard the wailing of women long before they arrived back at the wagon circle. Later, as they soberly threaded their way back inside where lanterns were lighted, people moving boldly back and forth, children standing, big-eyed and solemn here and there, and with a faint, far-away pale streak against the starry horizon, several immigrant men came forth to peer at Eli's returning party and take charge of their horses.

Jess felt an insistent little plucking at his sleeve and turned. It was Jonathan, looking grave. He leaned forward to whisper. "Two womenfolk was found dead under the wagons. Three more got wounds. How many men did they lose?" Jess told him and Jonathan nodded softly as though to say it was not an exorbitant cost, but neither was it a welcome one.

Peggy Wheelock came up and halted in front of Potter Houston. "Are you all right?" she asked. He nodded down at her. She held up a hand. There was a tin cup in it. Potter took the cup gratefully and sipped. The others saw him swiftly blink. It wasn't coffee in that cup, it was raw whiskey.

The Missourians began drifting away with their womenfolk. A long, grim night was ended. Come daylight they'd go out and count the dead Comancheros. They would bury them; it was their Christian duty, but they would not say a good word over the graves.

Jess and his men went to their wagon, got their bedrolls, and tossed them down. They scarcely spoke at all. They had been very fortunate; not one of them was even nicked.

IX

The entire ensuing day was spent in camp. Jess and Gabe rode out to make a huge circle and see where the cattle were. They deliberately avoided that northward two-mile stretch where the fight had taken place, and by mid-afternoon were back in sight of the wagon circle again. Jeb loped out to meet them. He related that the immigrants had spent the day in mourning for their dead, caring for their injured, and in bleakly burying the renegades. He asked about the herd.

"Driftin' some," said Jess. "Impatient to get on northward into better grass. We'll lie over tonight and light out early tomorrow."

"Well," Jeb said, "I don't know about Potter." When Jess and black Gabe gazed at him, Jeb shrugged. "He 'n' that Miss Peggy been talkin' a lot together. I figure . . . an' so does Jonathan . . .

maybe Potter'll join up with the immigrants and go along southward."

Gabriel shook his head at that statement. "Naw, suh," he contradicted young Jeb. "Naw, suh, I don't believe that. He wouldn't leave us short-handed. I know them Houstons. They know where a man's duty lies."

Gabe, as it turned out, was shrewdly correct. Later, when the Texans were eating supper beside their wagon, silent as mice and awaiting Potter's decision, he heaved a mighty sigh and said to Jess: "Pull stakes in the mornin'?" And when Jess nodded, he said: "I've heard it said a man always leaves something behind when he goes up the trail that'll pull him back to Texas. I reckon that's true enough. How many more days you reckon it'll take, Jess?"

The others knew that Potter Houston, who'd been up the trail as often as Jess, knew exactly how long it'd take. Still, Jess said quietly: "Thirty more days. But, hell, Potter, you don't have to go. I'll hire one of the Missourians. You can go on back with. . . ."

"I said I'd push longhorns to the Kansas plains," Potter said shortly. "So I'll push 'em to the Kansas plains." He put aside his plate and looked around at them all. "But thanks for makin' the offer anyway." He leaned back and stared far off, closing himself away from them. Jess thought he understood Potter's sentiments. This was a hard, perilous existence; when something as promising as rare love came to a man when he'd just about despaired of it ever happening to him, it was mortal hard for him to leave it.

Eli Young came down in the late evening to sit with them. Wayne Levitt and Harper Ellis strolled out to see to their stock. Jonathan and Gabe stood back by the tailgate having a smoke and young Jeb followed Potter when the older men went purposefully walking over among the wagons.

Eli stroked his beard with bent fingers and stared into the little dying supper fire. "I know you figured I was sacrificin' our womenfolk and young 'uns when we rode out last night, Mister Howard, but I couldn't take the time to explain that I've been drillin' and practicin' these folks for just such a thing as happened last night. Womenfolk and young 'uns included."

"It made a difference," Jess dryly observed. "In fact, one of your women saved Wayne Levitt when a bronco buck tried to jump beneath a wagon."

"Well," said old Eli softly, "that's fine. An' as a matter of fact it's about him I come down to set with you this evening."

Eli finished rough-combing his beard and lifted his eyes. Jess, sensing something in the older man's grave expression, said: "Wayne? You mean he's done something?"

"No. Well, not exactly. What I mean, Mister Howard, is that no man who fought as well and bravely in defense of me 'n' mine as Levitt did last night is wholly bad in my eyes."

"Bad?" echoed Jess. "Come to the point, Eli."

"Aye, that I will, Mister Howard." Old Eli settled his back against a wagon wheel. "Some of my people recognized Levitt yesterday. But then, there was no time. Besides, Levitt wasn't important right then. Today, though, it's different."

"What's different?"

"I see you don't know Wayne Levitt, Mister Howard."

"I know him," insisted Jess. "He's a top hand with longhorns an' he holds up his end of the other work. On top of that he can fight right well."

"Yes," assented old Eli. "An' if you take him up onto the Kansas plains, bein' as loyal to one another as you Texans are, you may die up there defending him. Wayne Levitt's wanted for murder in Missouri, Mister Howard. He shot and killed a bank messenger two years back. He got three thousand dollars in gold and disappeared. All folks knew was that he was one of those Texas trail hands. But last year he was identified by name and posters were put up offering five hundred dollars for information about him."

Jess felt in a pocket for his makings. To avoid looking at old Eli for a moment, he dropped his head for as long as it took to manufacture and light a cigarette. "You plumb certain it's the same man?" he eventually asked.

130

"Plumb certain, Mister Howard. I've seen those posters myself. So have others in my party. It's the same man, all right. Even the same name. That puzzled us for a spell, then we figured, him bein' a Texan and down in Texas he'd be safe enough among his own folks. Yes, sir, I'm plumb certain. So are five of my men." Eli looked out and around, then back toward the little dying fire again. "But we've talked on it," he murmured. "We will not ever mention knowing him. When a man, even a wanted man, risks his life for your womenfolk and young 'uns, the least you can do is forget, isn't it?"

"I reckon it is," muttered Jess, recalling all the times Wayne had drifted away when strangers had come to their camps, how he kept to himself, and how, as Jonathan had once observed, he never wholly relaxed.

"The money," stated Eli. "Well, the money's a powerful temptation any time, I expect. But killing . . . that's something us folks don't much cotton to except in defense of us and our'n. You understand?"

Jess nodded, drew a deep down sweep of smoke, and slowly exhaled it. "Why did he sign on with me to go back up north, I wonder," he mused aloud. "Are those posters in Kansas, too?"

"They are. Maybe Wayne doesn't know that. Maybe he figures after two years folks have forgotten. But they haven't, and I reckon you men know there are some of the toughest lawmen in the West up there in those Kansas cow towns. For five hundred dollars they'd shoot down Wayne Levitt on sight."

"I'm obliged for your visit," said Jess as Jeb came strolling back to join Jonathan and Gabe at the tailgate of their wagon. "We'll be pullin' out before sunup in the morning. Someday we'll likely meet again, Eli." Jess pushed out his hand. The older man gripped it, pumped once, and let go.

He said: "There's one more thing. My niece and Potter Houston."

Jess was mildly surprised. "I didn't know she was your niece."

"My sister's child, Mister Howard. Her mother died of the fever in Missouri some years back. Her pappy was killed in the war at the Wilderness. I keep wonderin' about them. Your man . . . with his saber scar . . . he made it right plain when we first met he didn't like Yankees."

Jess nodded over that, but with a loose little tolerant smile down around his lips. "He's met his match the rest of us figure, Eli. Miss Peggy's just about the only woman I've ever seen that could put the ring in Potter Houston's nose. I figure he knows that, too. Anyway, he's goin' on up to the Kansas plains with us. That'll give them both plenty of time to think things through. But one way or another, I can tell you he's a good man. Strong and smart and brave."

"Honest, Mister Howard?" Old Eli asked, gazing down his nose at Jess. "Honest and truthful?"

"Both honest and truthful. The war left more than just that external scar. I'll bet you a new saddle your niece can heal the internal one like no one else ever could."

Eli heaved up to his feet, shook Jess's hand again, and departed. Jonathan looked around the tailgate and said he was going to throw out the last of the coffee unless Jess helped drink it. Jess sauntered on around where Jonathan and Gabe and Jeb were lounging in the dying day. Wayne Levitt came strolling up to join them. A little later so also did Harper Ellis. They talked a little and finished the coffee. Jess had another smoke. He'd been out to the herd, their horses were ready, even the wagon was pointed in the right direction—northward. Nothing was left to be cared for.

"We'll roll out ahead of dawn," he told them. "With any kind of luck we ought to be out of this damned country by tomorrow night." He left them to hunt up his blankets. That coffee had been as strong as acid so he had a bitter taste in his mouth, but, as he lay back and composed himself inside the gloomy, quiet wagon circle, he was only indifferently aware of the taste.

How, he wondered, did a man say to another man that the murder he'd committed two years earlier had not been forgotten or forgiven, and that, if he went on up to the Kansas country, he was very likely to be arrested or killed?

A lanky shadow came silently over and hunkered

near Jess's bedroll. He turned his head and met that black, steady stare of Potter Houston. Some sixth sense told him Potter also knew about Wayne Levitt. "All right," he muttered, low and soft. "Spit it out."

Potter nodded. "Wayne," he replied. "Peggy told me. You knew?"

"Not until an hour ago I didn't. Eli came visitin'."

"Well," said Potter, "what do we do . . . tell him he's been recognized?"

"No. Eli said the Yanks won't turn him in. Anyway, they're heading in the wrong direction to get him into much trouble."

"Yeah, but up in Kansas, Peggy said, there are posters. We can't leave him t' ride up there and get killed."

"I was just wondering about that, Potter."

"You could fire him, Jess."

"We've been ridin' short-handed as it is. We need him."

"Badly enough to get him killed, Jess?"

"I'll be damned if I know what to do. Maybe fire him after we're just barely over the line."

"Naw, hell. He'd go for the nearest town, which would be a Kansas settlement. He wouldn't stand a chance."

Jess heaved up onto one elbow and looked around the silent camp. Armed sentries paced here and there, several lanterns burned, the corralled livestock shuffled around, there were a number of little dying fires where immigrant families had cooked supper.

"We don't have to decide tonight," Jess eventually said. "It'll be a week, maybe two weeks, before we hit the plains country. We'll come up with something before then."

"I hope so," said Potter, and straightened back as though to arise. "By the way, as soon as we've gotten paid for the beef and you divvy up the wages, I'll be headin' straight back."

Jess nodded. A brief twinge of jealousy passed over him.

"You ugly devil, Potter, how'd she ever pick you?"

Houston hung there, giving Jess that black, dead-level stare of his for a moment, then he slyly grinned and said: "Well, now, I'll tell you, Texas. She's just a topnotch picker of men is all." He stood up and, still grinning, started away.

Jess watched him walk away thinking that maybe, just maybe, she was at that. Potter had his bad side, just like every other living man had, but he had a good side that was far greater.

It was odd how destiny paired up a man and his woman sometimes; Potter Houston, with his deep-down resentment of Yankees, was going to marry one. She, on the other hand, had lost her father to Rebel soldiers; whether she hated ex-Confederates or not Jess had no idea, but she sure had cause to.

135

Yet of them all, she'd picked the foremost ex-Rebel among them all, and for some strange reason neither of them seemed to see in the other any vestige of an old enemy at all. He lay back again, sighed, and watched the stars flash and wane and flash again. Somewhere, he told himself, there was a Peggy Wheelock heading down the trail toward a meeting with him. Maybe she'd be a Yankee, too. But since he had much less of that old antipathy, he only softly smiled at the thought. Maybe that was why men fought wars—slowly to bring together all the divisions of mankind. It seemed a right odd way to achieve it, but sure enough after each conflict old enemies became new friends.

He closed his eyes. Dawn would come too soon as it was. Thirty more days to go and only the Lord knew what it held and He surely wouldn't tell a man.

X

There were precious few immigrants up and stirring when the Texans broke camp, heaved bedrolls into Jonathan's wagon, got astride in the chilly pre-dawn to fan out east and west to begin their northward push. A little pigtailed girl with her face scrubbed so that it shone peeped from under wagon canvas as Jess passed by. She didn't call to him but her large eyes darkened with a solemn sadness, and she watched him out of sight.

Her first love had just come and gone. As she grew older, there would be other loves, even greater ones, but never again one so bittersweet as this one.

Potter turned once just before the wagons fell away in the pre-dawn gloom. Then he, too, rode on without looking back again.

As though to compensate for their earlier troubles, Nature sent a pleasant morning that faded into a red-glazed pleasant afternoon. She withheld her winds and clouds and other inconveniences. by evening, she even put the cattle on the edge of a lush grass meadow a thousand acres in size that was scooped out of the harsher plain. A perfect bedding ground for tired men and hungry animals.

Potter volunteered for first night watch because he couldn't have slept anyway, and black Gabe spelled him off at 11:00. Jeb and Wayne finished the watch. Wayne was the last one in. The ensuing dawn broke, when cookie sent up his breakfast smoke, traditional manner for calling in night hawks.

The second day was just as bland, just as warmly agreeable and uneventful. They nooned near a red-clay cutbank near an old Indian burial ground, and afterward skirted the place, heading toward a distant dark bluff of land that cut directly across in front of them. That bluff looked to be a barrier to progress for the critters but it wasn't. Potter loped to the point and led the bell steer around and

through a narrow break—called by Mexican cow-boys *cañon de muerto* because inside its dark and narrow depths a large pack train had once been completely destroyed down to the last pack mule and *arriero* by Comancheros—but Potter led the longhorns through, then dropped off on the other side of the pass and waited for Jess. Ahead of them lay a flatness that stretched to the end of the earth. Now and then a very low hill rose up here and there, but not often. They were nearing the plains country. In fact, for seven days they drifted across a sea of grass mottled by cloud shadows, dwarfed to ant size, and held down to a snail pace gait because the longhorns grazed as they went along.

There were antelope aplenty but they didn't shoot any for the simple reason that the antelope saw the men before the men could get into gun range, and, as for running antelope down on a horse, even men from the brush country of Texas knew better than to try that. Nothing could catch running antelope.

The way to get camp meat in antelope country was to hang a white rag on a bush or a stick poked into the ground, then lie belly down in the tall grass and wait. It might take all day but eventually the curious little critters would sidle up to sniff the cloth. Jonathan, when asked by Jeb if he wanted some antelope meat, turned up his nose. "Not one you'd shoot," he answered. "If you gut-shoot an antelope, there's only one thing that stinks worse,

an' that's a gut-shot deer with a bellyful of fermentin' acorns. No, sir, you just never mind bringin' me any part of one o' them fancy goats. That's Injun meat."

This tremendous prairie country had once been the heartland of Comanchería—land of the Comanche Indians. They were gone now but there was plenty of sign around to show that for a thousand years they'd been here. Burial grounds, old stone rings where the camps had been. Broken tools and weapons, the burned places where they'd cleared ground. And wild horses.

It was the mustangs that could cause a big drive of longhorns no end of trouble. Flighty, racing wild horses had caused more than one wild stampede, so the Texans rode with their weapons ready and with their heads up and moving. They would drive away any mustangs that happened along before the cattle got spooked by them.

But it didn't happen; no stampede, no trouble of any kind until they were following over the curve of the distant land onto the Kansas plains, and even then it wasn't the kind of trouble they were alert to—man-made trouble. It was a steady build up of dirty clouds drifting down from the north, and another army of clouds scudding in from the east. Those two storm fronts would meet just about overhead of the herd half way out of Texas onto the Kansas plains.

Thundershowers were far from a rarity up on the

plains but that didn't make them any more welcome to Texas drovers. If just rain and wind came, it wasn't too bad, but sometimes there was thunder like giants rolling huge barrels through a vaulted dungeon, and that sound could almost be depended upon to frighten longhorns.

Jonathan kept a worried eye upon the clouds as he tooled the wagon along, and his interest was sharper than the anxiety of the riders; a *cocinero*'s charge was the camp wagon. It was a clumsy, laden vehicle. Horsemen could race away from a stampede and usually make it. *Cocineros*, with less speed and maneuverability, very often, if the herd happened to reverse itself in panic and run southward, got upset or killed. As old Jonathan had once told young Jeb, a stampede was just about the only way a Texas drover ever got killed and buried at the same time, and, if he was held down by a wagon and team, it was just about a lead-pipe cinch that's what would happen if the herd turned back.

But the clouds seemed to halt up there, or at least to slow their inexorable headlong rush to a crawl, as evening came on. That didn't fool Wayne or Jonathan or Gabe or Potter, who'd been up the trail before. Or Jess, either, who dismounted at evening camp and made a slow, long study of the heavens. Before a storm there was almost always a warm, hushed lull. That's exactly what was over the land now, a great depth of hot silence. Horses' tails splayed out from static electricity. Harper Ellis told young Jeb to sleep with all his clothes on. Not to remove his boots no matter what else he did, because sometime in the night the storm would hit.

Their supper was a quiet one. There was a powerful menace in the darkness. Even when that half moon shone, it was diaphanous with a wetly reflected glow.

"Fetch in fresh horses," Jess ordered, "and keep 'em tied to the wagon. Jeb, you 'n' Gabe take first night watch. Jonathan, keep the coffee pot on the coals tonight but put everything else in the wagon."

Jonathan muttered under his breath and squatted by the fire like a witch, his grizzled hair awry, his face twisted with real concern. Harper sniffed with his big hooked beak and shook his head. There was that metallic scent to the night that definitely presaged a storm. "I hope the damned critters head north when they go," he growled.

"We can he'p them make up their minds," stated Gabe. "When the first clap of thunder comes, we hit 'em from behind, shootin' and a-hollerin'. That's what some boys does up on these plains."

Harper Ellis was restless. He walked out a way, then back again. "Gettin' blacker'n the inside of old Toby," he reported.

They bedded down early, the night hawks out with the herd, and Jonathan heaved their blanket rolls into the wagon. He was the last one to lie down. It was the waiting. It got to old Jonathan and kept him hobbling about the camp. In a situation like that it was always the waiting that was bad.

About 11:00 a low, moaning breeze came along, low and warm, to pass through, heading southward. Jonathan sniffed it, determined which direction it was traveling, and swore to himself because, if it thundered, the herd would in all probability follow the wind. He was considering going over to shake Jess awake and propose that they move camp a mile or two westerly when far away and softly rumbling like the firing of cannon came the first sounds of storm. Jonathan didn't have to awaken Jess; if he'd been asleep at all, he came wide awake the second that far-away mutter came down the night in its echoing growl. As he rolled out and clamped on his hat, Jess called to the others.

"Roll out and rig up! Jonathan, hitch your team! Get everything in the wagon."

His orders were sharp and minimal, the commands of a man who had been through this identical situation before. Everyone was moving in seconds because the first thunder was always followed by a second roll of it, usually closer as the storm advanced down the electrified night.

It didn't take them long to get ready. Wayne Levitt finished first so he lent a hand with Jonathan's team and the loading. Jess was the first one astride. "Shake a leg!" he called to the others.

"Jonathan, head west and keep going until you run out of it. Don't bother about the rest of us, just mind yourself and the wagon. Get moving!"

The second battery of distant cannon rumbled as Jonathan swung his horses and laid on the whip. Their wagon went *creaking* and bouncing due west with old Jonathan up there cursing the horses, the night, and the advancing chill that moved in just ahead of the storm. Jess and the others watched him go, then turned northward, their faces lifted into the pungent breeze where the strong scent of a thousand cattle was strong, riding slowly at first because they didn't know how the herd had been bedded.

Gabe came out of the gloom at a standing trot. He shook his head before he got close enough to speak, then he twisted and swung his arm northerly and eastward to indicate how the herd was standing. "All up now," he said. "Ain't none of 'em in their beds no more. Standin' up there, shakin' their cussed horns and rollin' their eyes. One big clap directly overhead'll do it."

"Where's Jeb?" someone asked.

Gabe pointed eastward again. "Left him off to the east a ways. Said he'd try 'n' turn the leaders northward when they broke."

Harper Ellis sniffed and peered ahead where the nearest cattle stood, hunched up with their wicked big horns pale in the growing darkness. Clouds moved raggedly in from the north and met banks of other clouds coming from the east. Where they met, roiled air swept along, chilling and turbulent. There was the feeling of lightning in the air but the Texans didn't heed that; lightning, if it crackled close, would also start the panicked rush of long-horns, but they worried less about that than the thunder because now the muffled rumble of giant drums began again, and much closer this time.

Finally the cattle began lowing and milling, sometimes striking horns and making a sharp, *clicking* sound when this occurred. The men looked at Jess. He was calm, up there in his saddle. Tense as coiled spring but calm in the face as he hauled out his carbine. The others followed that example. He knew exactly what to do but hesitated to do it. If some genuine miracle would occur and the stampede did not come off, there would be no need to start the cattle running. But that kind of hope, recurrent though it might be, was almost wholly futile. He looked around. They all sat there waiting for his signal.

He said: "Take care now. Stay behind 'em. Everyone set?"

Everyone was. Jess raised his carbine and fired. The others booted out their horses, making a wild rush at the nearest cattle, also firing. They were anticipating the next big clap of thunder. The nearest cattle, already teetering upon the edge of wild panic, bawled and lunged ahead striking other cattle as the Texans hit them on the run, firing and yelling. They had gauged it perfectly, for out of the west came a giant forked orange tongue of blinding light and an earthshaking roar of thunder that completely drowned out the gunshots. But the stampede was already under way.

They rode behind the cattle, controlling their frightened horses with the left hand, firing their weapons with the right hand, pushing the herd along so that its momentum would catch up all the onward cattle and send them along in the same direction.

It worked. Some longhorns, farther off to the west or east, ran pell-mell, but the great majority swept along northward making the earth quake underfoot, and making the gamy air strong with their sweaty smell.

More lightning came. More thunder, deafening peals of it that made it unnecessary for the Texans to rely any further on their guns. They rushed along through dust and darkness, yelling back and forth until they eventually got separated in the wild night. After that it was every man for himself.

As long as the herd raced northward, it was at least traveling in the right direction. There would, of course, be casualties; there always were. Some weak critter would stumble and a hundred would charge right over him. But at least Jonathan and their camp wagon were safe. The two perils now confronting the men were prairie-dog holes that could up-end a running horse, perhaps snap his leg and hurl his rider end over end into the herd, or the sudden, totally unpredictable reversing of a split-off segment of the herd that could run over a mounted man, knock him down, and kill both the man and his horse in seconds.

But these were seasoned drovers, following the herd. Potter and Jess and Harper Ellis, as well as Wayne Levitt and Gabe, had been through stampedes before. They took their risks but never unnecessarily. They sped along, being as careful as they could be, riding down the savage night, but never avoiding the risk to save their necks if it became mandatory that they lean toward the herd to keep it running straight northward.

Rain came. Not the gentle good rain of late spring that fell elsewhere, but the drenching sheets of cold, black water that carved fifty-foot-deep erosion gullies on the Great Plains. They had slickers aft on their cantles but had no time to put them on.

But rainfall meant the heart of the storm was sweeping up and past, so they welcomed that deluge even though it made the footing doubly dangerous for their horses as well as for the racing longhorns.

Finally they detected that the thunder was moving off; the lightning was losing its blue-blurred ferocity. Their particular storm was passing. There was a brisk coldness to the air that cut through each man's drenched clothing as he slackened off his speed a little and began to peer around for the others. They were widely separated, but what seemed oddest was that off in the dingy east a pale streak appeared. What had seemed to have lasted only a few hours had in fact lasted throughout the night.

If there had been broken country ahead, they could have lost half their herd in blind rushes over cliffs. A lot of things could've been worse than they were.

Jess finally halted his used-up mount near a shattered, solitary chaparral clump. He got stiffly down with his teeth chattering, gathered faggots, and coaxed up a little flame. The earth still shook but the sound and the fury steadily diminished as the longhorns sped away. He tried to make a smoke but the papers were wet, so he gave it up and squatted there, soaking up smoky warmth.

Potter was the first one to arrive, drawn by the little dancing flame. Wayne Levitt came up next on a limping horse. Harper was the last one to arrive. They asked each other about Gabe and young Jeb but had no answers. Still, there was no cause yet for alarm. Potter's cigarette papers were carried inside the sweatband of his hat. They were dry. They all had a smoke and crouched in closer to the fire, numbly silent and exhausted. It had been a long night and, before that, it had also been a long day.

"Every time I say it's the last time," said Harper Ellis, moodily staring into the fire. "An' every spring I sign on to go up the trail again. A man's got to be a damned fool to keep it up."

XI

It was Gabriel who rode in at dawn to tell them young Jeb was dead. They hadn't yet seen hide nor hair of Jonathan or the wagon and Wayne Levitt was afoot because his mount had twisted its ankle on the rain-slippery ground, but they all at once started back with Gabe, Wayne on foot until Jess took him up behind his saddle.

There was no dust at all; the air was clean and fresh and turning warm. They were dirty, crumpled, unshaven, and sore-eyed. Their animals hung their heads. Somewhere miles ahead were the longhorns, run out now and probably grazing, although they could not be seen from where the Texans halted and stiffly got down.

Gabe had read the sign when he'd found the body of the youngest Texan and his trampled horse. He pointed it out to the others. "Went down after the rain 'cause them tracks is clean. His horse stumbled. There's the mud on his knee and on his nose. He lurched to catch his balance and fell plumb in front o' the critters."

Jeb was trampled flat. One boot was torn off, one rain-washed foot pale blue in the dawn light. He

was face down, hatless, and filthy. It looked as
though several hundred cattle had gone over him.
He was pressed out a foot wider than he'd been in
life. His horse had been squashed, too, disembow-
eled. The ground was a red-rusty color.

They had no tools. Jess stood silently for a spell
then said: "Wayne, go find Jonathan and fetch the
wagon up here." He turned to Harper Ellis and
Potter Houston. "You fellers jog north an' locate
the herd. Count the dead ones as you go. The wagon'll be here when you get back."

The men parted, leaving Gabe and Jess with the
body. Old Gabe sniffled and dragged a torn sleeve
across under his nose. "The song say . . . 'He won't
see his mother when the work's all done this fall',
Mistah Jess. It sure Lord tells the truth. He was
mighty powerful young t' die."

"He shouldn't have been in so close, Gabe."

"No. But he was a young 'un. He didn't know.
You know how it be with young 'uns. Everythin'
they got to do carries the weight of the world with
it. Them cussed cattle'd have gone on anyway, but
he had to make plumb sure. He was the on'y one
up here in the lead. He figured the full responsibility was his."

"You know his folks, Gabe?"

"Yas, suh. Down in Sweetwater."

"Yeah. Fine folk. He was their only child. Gabe,
I don't feel so good."

"No man'd feel good. It's been a powerful long

149

night." Gabe bent to straighten a shattered arm and a grotesquely twisted leg. "Never see a dead one I don't get to speculatin'. Take young Jeb here. Mistah Jess, he knows somethin' now don't none of us know."

Jess went over to his horse and fished in a saddle pocket, found what he wanted—a fresh, dry packet of cigarette papers—and made a smoke for breakfast. Far off someone called out. The sound rang bell-clear down across the sparkling distance. Wayne Levitt was coming along on horseback ahead of Jonathan's wagon. Wayne had ridden Gabe's horse, and, as Gabriel saw him coming, he remained squatting beside the body, just watching. There was a bluish grayness around Gabe's eyes where the flesh sagged from weariness. He struggled back upright as the wagon wheeled in close and halted. Jonathan stiffly clambered down and wordlessly hobbled over to gaze down at young Jeb. Then he went back and rummaged inside the wagon for shovels. He handed one to Jess, one to Gabe. He returned to the wagon, still without speaking to anyone, got some clean rags, and went back to wipe young Jeb's face and hands.

While the digging went on, with Wayne taking turns with the others, Jonathan brought forth a bag of cow chips and set about making a fire. For an hour each man worked without saying anything to the others, but when it was time to roll Jeb in his blankets and put him into the hole, Jonathan clambered inside the wagon, squirreled around in there with much grunting, and crawled back out with a dog-eared copy of the Good Book. He read the prayer as Wayne and Jess shoveled back the dirt. Gabe stood bareheaded, humped, and saddened.

The sun turned hot. The atmosphere was unnervingly humid after that rain. They drank coffee and finished rounding off the grave. They put up no marker of any kind, not even a wooden cross. Their reason was elemental; roving bands of Indians made a habit of plundering graves for the pants and shirts and boots. Such an indignity would not befall young Jeb; within a year or so even the men who'd buried him wouldn't be able to return to this spot with accuracy.

They had his spurs, gun, and gun belt, his pocket watch, and his pathetic other valuables tied neatly in a bundle made of his neckerchief. Those things would eventually be delivered to his parents down at Sweetwater by Jess Howard, along with the story of how he had died. That was the range boss's job.

Potter and Harper Ellis drifted back before evening. The herd, they reported, standing there gazing at the grave, was about seven miles upcountry, spread out for five miles but content to stand now, having exhausted itself.

"Thirty-six dead ones," Potter said to Jess, "that we passed, and six more we had to shoot for busted legs and what-not. Total loss of forty-two head."

It was a very low figure, but none of them said anything about it. They had an early supper and bedded down. This would be the last camp they'd share with Jeb. None of them bothered taking the night watch and Jess didn't even suggest it. There wasn't much need anyway; the only trouble that could sneak up in the night would be renegades, and that wasn't very likely.

At dawn Jonathan fed them fried salt beef, black coffee, and sourdough bread, then they struck out northward in search of the herd. They sighted part of it by noon and scattered out to bring it together. This was not completely accomplished that day, so they spent the next day finishing up, had an early supper beside a little muddy stream, and before dawn were once more on the way.

Now, except that young Jeb was not there, the drive went on as before; dust rose up, cattle got irritable, flies plagued them all, cattle, horses, and men; the heat became a solid force they had to buck into head-on as they crossed the last immense flat stretch of prairie. At camp on the Kaw River the sixth night after leaving young Jeb, Jess said to Wayne Levitt: "Take a walk with me out to look at that horse you rode the night of the stampede. I think his ankle's about healed." A hundred yards from the wagon where their rope corral had been set up to contain their saddle animals, Jess turned his back on the horses and said: "Wayne, I got to tell you something. We're in Kansas now. The next state up the line is Missouri. You've been up there before, I reckon."

Wayne was standing quite still, eyeing Jess's darkly weathered face with a gathering intentness. "I've been in Missouri before," he said, "a couple of times."

"Well, things that happened up there a couple of years back, Wayne, aren't forgotten. In fact, I got it on real good authority they're just about as well known down here in Kansas now."

Wayne's expression was smoothly taut. "Meaning . . . ?" he murmured.

Jess took in a big breath. "Three thousand in gold coin and a dead man, Wayne. They've got posters in Kansas offerin' five hundred. The posters have your picture on them."

"Who told you that?"

"Eli Young."

"Oh," said Wayne, and subsided for a thoughtful long moment. "He recognized me?"

"Yeah. But he said he an' his folks owed you something."

"Five hundred reward is a lot of money, Jess."

"It is for a fact. A year's wages in some places."

"Do the other fellers know, too?"

Jess thought of Potter and shrugged. "That's not what's troublin' me, Wayne. If you go anywhere near one of the settlements up here, some sod-buster's going to try an' collect that five hundred reward. And this isn't Texas. Folks in Kansas got no love for Texans."

"Damned Yankees," growled Levitt, running the words together.

"You'd better pull out, Wayne. If you go the rest of the way, there'll be bad trouble sure as you're a foot high."

Levitt stepped over and gazed past the grazing horses. For a long time he stood in thought, but eventually he faced Jess again. "I lost half that money in a poker game in Wichita. The other half I sent to my folks down at Eagle Pass. My paw's crippled up from the belt down from a hunk of steel in the war. Jess, I didn't mean to shoot that man. He had a little Derringer in his palm and tried to use it."

"Sometimes," murmured Jess vaguely, "things work out that way, Wayne. You've been a good man on this drive. One of the best. I've got some money in my bedroll. I'll pay you off tonight. By mornin' you'd best be long gone. Don't head for one of the settlements up here. I know how dry a man gets on a drive, but don't do it. Head back for Texas. I'll give you the money after the others have bedded down. All right?"

"I reckon, Jess. Dammit all, for the first time in a couple of years I've felt like I used to feel . . . free and able to relax among folks. I reckon I'll always be runnin' from that."

"About a horse," said Jess, turning to gaze into

154

the rope corral. "Take one of the other ones. Yours needs another few weeks of rest before that ankle'll get sound again. If you had to run for any reason an' were ridin' him, he'd go lame on you sure."

Wayne nodded and put out a hand. "I'm obliged, Jess. You tell Potter an' Harper an' Gabe for me. And old Jonathan, too. You do that for me, will you?"

"Sure. Well, I'll go back to camp. You stay around out here for a spell if you like."

Jess walked away, leaving Levitt back there in the soft-lighted balmy night. There was nearly a full moon now, big and lopsided and silent in a high overhead crossing. The land lay silvery unless a little breeze came along, then grass heads swayed and rippled, making the silver turn a green-blue shade in the darkness.

Jonathan was chopping jerky to make into a stew when Jess returned without Wayne Levitt. They exchanged a look and a nod. Harper Ellis and Gabe were playing fan-tan on a blanket by firelight while Potter Houston sat by himself near the rear wagon wheel. He was holding an unlighted cigarette between his fingers, staring out into the vastness. Jess dropped down, made a smoke for himself, and held the match. Potter leaned into it. Afterward, as he exhaled, he whispered: "You told him."

Jess nodded.

"Good. Will he head back?"

"I told him to do that. He'll pull out sometime tonight."

Potter smoked a moment, then said with a comfortable sigh: "I been sittin' here thinking. You know, Jess, the Longhorn Trail changes men. It's like war. You may only go through it once but ever afterward you're changed. Why should that be? A man ordinarily lives a long time after he's made the drive, a heap of other things happen to him afterward, but they don't affect him the same way. I'm not talkin' about young Jeb. I'm talkin' about the rest of us. The trail changes us some more each time we go up it. What is it that makes it so? You got any idea?"

Jess trimmed ash from his cigarette and tossed aside his hat as he eased big shoulders back against the same wagon wheel. "It's a lot of life an' livin' capsuled up into a couple of raw months, Potter. Millions of men live fifty, sixty years an' never go through half what we go through between the Sweetwater and the Wichita. Comancheros, settlers, storms, stampedes, an outlaw amongst us, and tomorrow somethin' else, all of it cruel and savage. Sure it changes men. If it didn't change 'em . . . make 'em more alert and aware . . . it'd kill 'em." Jess inhaled, exhaled, changed his tone a little, and added: "You . . . now you'll head on back and find where she's settled, which is how it ought to be. You'll raise up sons and you'll grow old in

156

Texas where you belong. And you'll think back to this drive . . . to young Jeb and Wayne and black Gabe and the rest of us. But you'll never go up the trail again. Still, it'll have left its indelible mark on you, Potter. It does it to all of us, because it's a heap of raw livin' crammed into a damned short space of a man's lifetime. Now, we'd better bed down. From tomorrow on we'll be *two* riders short. That means twice as much ridin' for the rest of us. Good night."

Potter watched Jess stand up. "Good night," he said, and sat on after Jess had headed for his blanket roll, moodily smoking and thinking.

XII

Wayne's departure in the night surprised Jonathan and Harper Ellis. They were condemnatory, too, around the breakfast fire, until Jess told them the whole story. Then Jonathan said exultantly: "I told you, Jess Howard. I told you back before them Comancheros showed up, he was some sort of feller on the dodge."

Potter gazed up at Jonathan from where he hunkered. He said nothing, just looked up. Jess finished eating, tossed his plate into the bucket, and drank another cup of java. It was chilly before dawn. Unreasonably chilly, because two hours after sunup it would be hotter than the inside of a bean pot.

"Come on," he ultimately said to Potter and Harper Ellis, and led out to where the horses and saddles were. They rigged out and rode off separately, Jess to the east, Harper to the west, and Potter straight ahead northward. Behind them Jonathan went about breaking camp, hitching the team, and pulling out. Even being crippled in the legs like he was didn't seem to slow old Jonathan, and, since he talked to himself briskly all the time he was working, he was usually in fairly good company. At least there were blessed few arguments.

The sun steadily climbed. It changed from fresh golden to malevolent lemon-yellow. Tan-colored dust began coming to life. The cattle, gaunted still from their wild night and the subsequent days of being pushed hard to keep them tired, walked along almost indifferently. Once a pair of bulls locked horns, but their hearts really weren't in it. Another time a wolf—probably deaf—sprang up out of a little arroyo where he'd possibly been catnapping and, in panic at finding men around him, broke through the herd, scattering cattle for a half mile. Potter and Jess swore at him; either one of them could have shot the blasted creature, but they didn't. It took enough time to get the startled critters back into the herd again as it was; firing a gun from behind them wouldn't have improved anything.

The old wolf ran away, mangy, sly-eyed, tongue

lolling, the picture of a lobo full of years. No need to shoot him anyway, really; one more winter of deep snow and old as he was, he'd perish. Nature had her own way of thinning out varmints.

Late in the afternoon they sighted a spiral of dust moving southward. It was well east of them as though perhaps there might be a stage road over yonder. Or possibly a cow outfit where the hired riders were returning before suppertime. Jess recalled no such road or ranch, but then he wasn't actually familiar with all Kansas anyway.

They made their camp in a grassy swale a mile westerly to avoid all the settling dust. There were longhorns strung out upcountry for quite a distance. While the others washed down and cared for their saddle stock, Jess made a big sashay northward. His was the first herd onto the plains this spring, and yet a man never knew. Sometimes Kansas speculators bought the full herds and wintered them through, hoping to make a killing in early spring. Sometimes they hit it; sometimes they didn't. If they didn't, their herds would be scattered all over creation. The danger of a mix-up was to be avoided at all costs; it could hold up a herd's departure on the cars as much as two weeks while the Kansas critters were being cut out, and meanwhile some other Texas herd could come up onto the plain and sell for top dollar.

He rode until just before sunset but saw nothing. At least he saw no cattle, but that whirling dust cloud was still off in the east. Only it seemed now to be coming westerly toward the herd. It was men on horses, there could be little doubt of that, so he didn't worry. They'd veer off somewhere along their route.

He rode on back to the camp.

Jonathan had outdone himself. As a surprise for them, he'd made a pie of dried apples with a baking soda crust. He saved this until they'd finished supper and were on their second cups of coffee, then brought it forth, preening like a peacock. They were properly surprised and pleased. Gabe said it was without question one of the best apple pies he'd ever eaten. Harper and Potter Houston smacked their lips and smiled. Any kind of sweetening was a genuine luxury on the trail. Old Jonathan basked in their appreciation like a *prima donna*. He described all the intricacies of making apple pie on the trail in minutest detail, and might have ended up getting deflated when the men got enough, except that somewhere out in the silvery dark a man sang out a loud halloo. Every one of them was instantly alert and wary. They sprang up, moving clear of the outlining fire. Even Jonathan hobbled around to the wagon's off side and surreptitiously reached under canvas for his shotgun.

They were close to several Kansas towns. There was Hemphill and Douglas and Prineville to the northeast, all villages actually, but still with people

160

in them and all the Kansas vestiges of civilization. The Texans only very indifferently knew these smaller towns; their goal had always been Wichita or Kansas City where the cattle buyers and railroad yards were. But once in a while, when thirst became unbearable, they had loped into some of those lesser places.

Jess said: "Probably riders from one of the easterly towns, but keep sharp watch anyway while I walk out there." He answered that earlier shout and invited the strangers to ride on up. They did, nine of them, all riding sweaty animals as though they'd come some little distance. It dawned on Jess as he made them out, walking their mounts up closer to Jonathan's fire, that these were the riders who'd been making all that dust off in the east.

When the nine men halted, one black-bearded bulky man out front with a coat on and a lawman's star pinned to the front of it settled down in his saddle and peered down at Jess from beneath a curled hat brim. "This here the Howard herd?" he asked. Jess said it was, that he was Jess Howard. The heavy man looked around again. He couldn't have failed to see the dull reflection of firelight off gun barrels here and there beyond the fire but he gave no hint of it. "Mind if we get down?" he asked.

"Don't mind at all," stated Jess, retreating back by the fire. "There's cups and there's coffee."

The men stepped down and moved forward,

leading their horses. They were a solemn lot, silent as stone and leery-eyed. The bulky man removed his gloves, stuffed them into a coat pocket, and said: "Mister Howard, I'm Sheriff Tom Meek from Prineville." He paused to stoop, fill a cup with coffee, and straighten up again. "I'm not here to cause you no trouble. Your boys can step around in plain sight."

"Sure," said Jess. "Potter, Harper, Jonathan come on out and have some coffee. You, too, Gabe. Come on around here."

Jonathan stepped out first, still holding the shotgun. He made a little sniffing sound and peered suspiciously at the men from Prineville. "There ain't that much coffee left," he mumbled, but he came forward anyway. So did Potter and Harper, their six-guns holstered, their faces swept clean of any expression at all.

There was very often trouble between Kansans and Texans. At the best, there was no comradeship between them, so the four Texans stood there across their little fire stonily eyeing the nine Kansans. Sheriff Meek motioned his men forward to get coffee, but only six of them moved; the last three remained where they were, watching the Texans.

"Pretty big herd you got out there," Meek said, holding his coffee cup in both hands as though to warm his palms and fingers. "Looks like maybe a thousand head."

"Less a few," replied Jess. "We lost about a hundred back some distance in a stampede."

"Kind of early up the trail, aren't you, Mister Howard?"

"Yeah. First up usually get a good price."

Sheriff Meek swished his coffee and nodded sympathetically. "Goin' to be a good year for the cattle, Mister Howard," he drawled very slowly, his thoughts obviously not on cattle drives at all. "But 'pears to me you don't have a very big crew for a thousand head. Three riders and the cookie."

"We lost a man in the stampede."

"That's too bad, Mister Howard. You only lost one man?"

"Just one, Sheriff."

Meek continued swishing his coffee and gazing down into the cup. "But you had another rider besides the one you lost when you left Texas, didn't you, Mister Howard?"

Jess hung fire. Jonathan made a lot of noise filling a cup with coffee. He said to the Kansans: "You boys back yonder there, you didn't get no java. Step right up. I can squeeze another three cups outen this old pot. Step up here, boys."

Under Jonathan's continued urgings the last three Kansans came forward and stiffly accepted their cups of coffee. They muttered thanks to old Jonathan and stepped away from the fire again. Jonathan beamed on them. "Nothing like hot, black coffee at the end of a long day, I always say."

163

Bulky, bearded Sheriff Meek soberly eyed Jonathan. He didn't interrupt; he just stood waiting for the chatter to end. When it did finally, he switched his attention back to Jess. "About that other rider," he said quietly. "I've got him in jail in Prineville, Mister Howard."

It became so quiet the faint and faraway bawl of a steer sounded bell-clear. The Texans were steadily regarding Sheriff Meek. Jonathan let his breath out softly but audibly. Jess leaned to put aside his coffee cup, still half full.

"What's his name, Sheriff?" he asked.

"You know it as well as I do, Mister Howard. It's Wayne Levitt. I'm not tryin' to put you on the spot at all. It's just that I know he come north with your drive. He made a bad mistake . . . two bad mistakes, to be correct about it. The first one was to ride into Prineville for a few drinks and the second mistake was to go for his gun when a deputy recognized him an' went up to arrest him."

Jess said: "He shot the deputy?"

Meek nodded. "He killed him, Mister Howard. That's one reason I got him in my jailhouse. The other reason, I expect you know. Because he's wanted for murder and robbery up in Missouri."

"Lord 'a' mercy," Gabe muttered as he stepped back to lean upon the forewheel of their camp wagon. Potter and Harper sagged a little. Jess hooked both thumbs in his shell belt and regarded Sheriff Meek.

164

"Why did you ride out here to tell me that?" he asked.

Meek looked around the camp as he said: "Well, mainly I reckon so's you'd know. But it never hurts to look over the Texas crews. Sometimes you boys get into trouble one spring, then ride back up here the following spring. You surely know how that is, Mister Howard."

Jess knew how it was but he didn't agree with Sheriff Meek. All he said was: "Wayne came up the trail with us, but none of my other men are wanted."

Meek eyed Harper Ellis and Potter Houston thoughtfully. "I'm right glad to hear that," he said, with no conviction at all in his voice. "There's another reason I came down here to see you fellers, though. That's because I figured you'd hear sooner or later Levitt was to be tried in Prineville. I thought maybe you bein' Texans, too, you might have some notion of helpin' him. Well, you're welcome in my territory any time. You can even speak up for Levitt at his trial, if you got anything to say. But things're goin' to be legal and orderly. That's why I got up this posse, Mister Howard, and back in town I got thirty more men armed and deputized. I don't want any trouble. I sure hope you feel the same way."

Potter Houston said: "Be pretty big odds, wouldn't it, Sheriff, forty men to four, ten to one?"

Meek nodded at Potter and kept watching the swarthy man's black gaze as it moved over his

165

posse men. "Be fatal odds," he murmured. "I'll promise you one thing. Levitt'll get a fair trial."

"And a neat hangin'," murmured Harper Ellis.

"Yes, that, too," agreed Sheriff Meek. "Boys, I don't judge 'em. That's for the judge an' jury to do. Levitt killed a law officer in the performance of his duty before a saloon full of witnesses. Besides that he's a wanted murderer. The case against him is strong. I know how it is when you been ridin' with a feller as long as you fellers rode with Wayne Levitt. I'm sorry. It would have pleased me right well if he hadn't shown up in my territory at all." Meek turned, fished out his gloves, and put them on, facing his horse. As he prepared to mount, he said: "Trial'll be tomorrow afternoon. You're welcome to sit in . . . but don't come to Prineville wearin' shootin' irons. Won't be any guns allowed in town durin' the trial except those bein' packed by deputized lawmen." Meek's heavy body settled across leather. His posse men also mounted up. For a moment longer the two groups eyed one another, then the Kansans turned and trotted stiffly back the way they had come.

With strong bitterness in his voice Jess said: "I told him not to head for one of those damned Kansas towns. I told him plain as day."

"Should've saved your breath," said Harper Ellis. "When a feller's been that long without a drink and he's close to one, he's goin' to have his liquor."

Potter put down his untouched cup of coffee and stepped back away from the fire to cock his head and listen to the diminishing beat of the Kansan horses out in the pewter night. He didn't say anything at all.

Gabriel didn't move off the wagon wheel as he watched Jess. Eventually he said: "Do we ride in there tomorrow?"

Jess fished for his tobacco sack, wearing a black scowl. "I reckon we do," he answered. "The least we can do is show Wayne he doesn't have to go out surrounded by strangers." He gave the cigarette a final savage twist and popped it between his lips. "The damned fool!"

Gabe went around where his blankets were and bedded down. The others lingered by Jonathan's fire a little while, looking gloomy and saying very little. Actually there wasn't much to say. The Kansans had Wayne and they'd hang him for killing their lawman. The Texans couldn't do a thing about it.

"Even," growled Jess, "if we had cause to. There's only one place to put the blame."

Potter agreed. So did Harper. But neither of them felt any the less gloomy over resolving that issue of blame. As Sheriff Meek had truthfully said, or had at least implied, when men rode together for as long as these men had, it made a difference what happened to one of them.

XIII

They rolled out two hours early the following morning so as to have ample time to make a sashay around the herd, making certain it would be all right, then they all headed for Prineville.

Jonathan was along. It hurt him to get astraddle a horse but sometimes that kind of physical pain was less than the mental anguish. He, like the others, was not wearing a pistol or shell belt. He had a Bowie knife in his boot scabbard but that hardly was being armed, at least not in the eyes of Texans who ordinarily were ambulatory arsenals on the trail. Anyway, Jonathan's trouser leg concealed the knife.

Prineville was a goodly distance northeastward from their wagon camp. The sun was high before they even came in sight of the place. It squatted out on the plain as though someone had just dropped it there. The houses were scattered and faced whichever direction their builders had fancied. There were five or six little crooked back roads, but the main thoroughfare lay east and west. It had stores its full length. There was a big set of community corrals north of town where, evidently, drovers penned their animals overnight while on the trail up to rail's end. At the south end of Prineville was the jailhouse, a sturdy, squat log building with recessed narrow little windows covered by steel gratings. It was toward this unmistakable edifice the Texans made their way as they walked their animals in off the prairie.

The place was bustling with activity and people. Men stood in small groups along the plank walks heatedly conversing. To Jess and his companions it was no secret what was being so ardently discussed. The townsmen who saw them enter town down near the jailhouse turned to stare impassively. It wasn't difficult to recognize Texas riders any time or any place. Unarmed ones were somewhat of a novelty, but this fact didn't seem to alleviate the sudden electrification that passed over those bystanders as the Texans drew rein before Tom Meek's jailhouse and got down. Instantly word sped up and down the town that a band of Texans had arrived.

Sheriff Meek, without his gloves and coat, was inside playing blackjack with his prisoner. He had three granite-faced deputized range riders in there with him, each man armed with a shotgun. When Jess walked in with Harper, Potter, Gabriel, and crippled Jonathan, the deputies straightened up and warily eyed them. Sheriff Meek lumbered to his feet. Beyond him, staring out of the strap-steel cage, Wayne Levitt's jaw sagged. Clearly Meek hadn't told Wayne the other Texans might be along.

Sheriff Meek nodded and ran an experienced eye up and down Jess first, then the others. "Any firearms?" he asked.

Jess shook his head. He was looking in at Wayne who was still holding a handful of playing cards. Jess said softly: "You ought to know better'n play blackjack with a sheriff." He smiled at the prisoner.

Levitt stood up and smiled back. "I'm winnin'," he said. "Took eleven cents off him so far." Levitt's smoky eyes ranged over the others and halted upon Jonathan. "You ride in or drive in?" he asked.

Jonathan grimaced and hobbled to a chair where he gingerly sat down. "I rode in. But it warn't no pleasure. Wayne, how do they feed you?"

"Not bad, Jonathan. Not bad." Wayne cleared his throat and ran a hand through his hair. "Guess I did the damn' fool thing, didn't I, fellers?"

No one replied to that but Potter said: "You got any tobacco?" He fished out a half full sack and offered it through the bars. Levitt took it. He had a purple discoloration alongside his jaw on the right side.

"Glad you fellers rode in," he said quietly, making a smoke.

Gabriel said: "They treatin' you all right?"

Wayne looked up and grinned a little. He and Gabe had been good friends on the trail. "Can't squawk too much, Gabe. They got no reason to love me, I reckon. You got a match?"

Gabe stepped over, held the light, and stepped back to snap it. Very softly he said: "Anythin' you want to send back, I'll take for you."

170

"Thanks," Wayne said, also speaking quietly. "Just the usual junk, Gabe. They got my guns and saddle an' stuff. They'll give it to you afterward, I reckon." He inhaled deeply, hungrily, and let the smoke out in a thin cloud of gray while he looked at them all, each in his turn. "Goin' to try me at one and hang me at two," he said. "They don't waste no time in Kansas, do they?"

Jess went over to Sheriff Meek. "Any objection to us buyin' him a good dinner and fetchin' it over here?" he inquired.

Meek said: "None at all, Mister Howard." Then he said: "But do me a favor . . . take a couple of my deputies with you over to the café. I know you won't like the idea, but like I told you last night, I don't want any more trouble, and folks are pretty roiled. That deputy was a good man."

Jess nodded and stepped back where Potter was standing. He fished out some coins and handed them to Houston. "The best they got," he said. "Enough for all of us."

Potter took the money and jerked his head at Harper. "I'll need help packin' it back," he said. "Come on."

Sheriff Meek sent two of his shotgun guards with the pair of lanky Texans. Not a word was exchanged between the Kansans who escorted them, and the Texans, all the while they were gone, and outside the jailhouse a big crowd was congregating. It may have been those shotguns or it may

171

have just been that the people were more curious than truculent, but nothing was said to Potter and Harper.

Jess and Gabe sat down on chairs outside Wayne's cell. Jonathan had already hitched his chair up close. He was fumbling with the cards Sheriff Meek had put down. He said: "What'n tarnation did you ride into this hole for anyway, Wayne? You should've knowed it was like walkin' into a bear's den."

Wayne nodded and avoided Jess's glance. "No excuse, Jonathan," he muttered. "Except I kept thinkin' about a couple of big shots of liquor."

"How many'd you have?"

Wayne grimaced. "I don't recollect, Jonathan. Must've been quite a few though, because I just barely recall the gunfight. This feller come at me reachin' for his Forty-Five. I didn't see his badge . . . at least I don't recollect seein' it. I just turned from the bar an' shot him. Then the damned lights went out. Meek told me later a feller cracked me alongside the jaw with his pistol barrel. Even that might not have been too bad except that they got posters around here on me. That cooked my goose."

Meek caught Jess's eye and jerked his head. Jess walked over. "Trial's due to start soon," the lawman said softly. "The judge come in on the morning stage. I think it'd be best if you fellers sat with me 'n' my men in the front row."

"Yeah," Jess said dryly, "it probably would at that. Tell me, Sheriff, has he any chance at all?"

Meek just looked Jess in the eye and said: "You know better'n that, Mister Howard." He then reached for his hat and put it on. "I got to go over an' help with the court. I'll leave three deputies here. When you fellers are through havin' dinner, they'll fetch you on over, along with the prisoner."

Sheriff Meek met Harper Ellis, Potter Houston, and their armed escorts at the door and stepped aside to allow them to enter with their baskets of food. He then spoke briefly with one of the guards, and passed on outside.

One of the shotgun guards helped set up a table outside Wayne's cell for the food, but the other two stood back frozen-faced; these two were hostile. They said nothing but they didn't have to, their expressions were enough.

Jonathan sniffed the food and grudgingly acknowledged that it was edible even though obviously prepared by Yankees. They all sat down and ate. There was a little chuckling, some banter when Gabe said he wasn't just sure which side of the bars he was on, and Wayne Levitt smiled often. Afterward, when the deputies said it was time to go and herded the other Texans away when they brought Levitt forth from his cage, the smiles got a little strained, the silences slightly longer and more awkward.

Outside, a big crowd was waiting. The Texans

with Jess walked out first. No one said anything although an audible mutter ran through the crowd. Then two shotgun guards, one on each side, appeared with Wayne Levitt, and a big blond-headed youth heaved his shoulders forward toward the front of the crowd and called Wayne a fighting name. Levitt turned instinctively and dropped his right hand. There was no gun there. One of the deputies wheeled and braced himself. When the onlooker came pushing through, the deputy raised his shotgun and cocked it. He and the angry man traded hard looks.

The deputy said: "Move back, Mike. You push for trouble an' there's goin' to be two funerals in your family. Get back now."

There was no mistaking the deputy's meaning at all. He would shoot. The man called Mike gave ground with a twisted look of fury across his face. Everyone breathed easier.

The courtroom was inside a saloon that had been cleared of patrons and had been re-arranged to make a very effective bar of justice. Sheriff Meck pointed where he wanted the prisoner. As Levitt went past Jess, he paused for just a second.

"I should've taken your advice. Well, anyway I'm right glad you fellers came to see me off. Good bye and good luck to all of you."

The guards frowned and Levitt moved on.

The room filled with people. Sheriff Meck pointed out where the Texans were to sit. The back wall was lined with armed special deputies. At each window and doorway stood a man with a riot-gun. The judge was a small, gray man behind the bar on a stool. He had a pistol and a law book on the counter in front of him. The lobe of one of his ears was gone, evidently shot off sometime. He scarcely let the spectators all get seated before he struck the counter with his .45 and declared the court in session. In swift succession he had witnesses sworn in and seated. There were no attorneys. The judge asked all questions and dismissed each witness when he was finished. When everyone but Wayne Levitt had been heard, he had Wayne sworn in, too, and seated, then he proceeded to pull the truth out of Wayne with little jabbing sentences. When he finally leaned back, finished with the accused, he fixed Levitt with a cold eye and said: "Young man, if you have anything to say in your own defense before I pass judgment . . . say it now."

Wayne looked from the judge to his former trail friends and back again. He shook his head at the judge. He had nothing more to say.

The judge picked up his six-gun, struck the bar top hard, put the gun aside, and leaned down gazing over the hushed room. "Guilty of murder in the first degree!" he exclaimed. "Sheriff, is your scaffold in working order?"

"It is, Your Honor."

"You will then take this prisoner hence and hang

him by the neck until he is dead, within one hour, and may God have mercy on his soul!"

A sigh resembling the stirrings of a faint breeze passed over the courtroom. Jess sat perfectly still. So did the others with him. Behind them people arose to file out; they muttered in low tones. Sheriff Meek came over and touched Wayne Levitt. As the prisoner arose, Meek slapped his right wrist with a steel cuff. He then led Levitt out of the courtroom with so many guards surrounding the Texan his former riding companions lost sight of the condemned man.

Gabriel muttered: "An' may God have mercy on his soul. Amen."

They finally also stood up to file out. The Kansans scarcely heeded them now, until they were passing outside, when a weasel-faced individual hissed at them: "Too bad it warn't the whole passel of you damned Texans." Potter Houston whipped around. So did Harper Ellis. But a townsman with a long arm reached over, caught the weasel-faced man by the shoulder, and wrenched him back out of harm's way. He then turned the smaller man, gave him a slight shove, and kicked him hard. The weasel-faced man squawked and went catapulting ahead. The Kansan turned to face Potter and Harper. "Always got to be one like that," he growled, then walked off with the rest of the crowd.

At the jailhouse Tom Meek stationed fifteen men

outside on the plank walk. Inside, he nervously manacled Wayne to a chair and let the other Texans sit with him for as long as it took to have a last smoke together. Levitt pulled out his watch and handed it to Gabriel with a crooked little grin.

"Remember, Gabe," he said, "tellin' me one night we were night hawkin', you didn't know how to tell time? Well, damn your old hide, now you got no reason for not learnin'."

Gabriel felt around for his big blue handkerchief and mightily blew his nose. "Sure smoky in here," he complained. "You fellers all puffin' away on them cigareets."

Sheriff Meek came over. "Time to go," he said to Wayne, and bent to unlock the cuff that was secured to the arm of Wayne's chair. As he straightened around with Wayne in tow, he said to his men: "Go out there and clear the damned side-walk. Clear it all the way to the scaffold."

The deputies stonily walked out, leaving the door open. People grumbled at being pushed back. Jess led his men out next. Behind them walked Sheriff Meek, sweating now until his shirt front was dark. He had Wayne.

The scaffold stood behind the jailhouse. It was a dazzling springtime afternoon. The crowd trooped along behind Meek's deputies entirely subdued. Meek finally turned, at the base of the scaffold, and gestured for his deputies to form a line. Directly behind it stood the four Texans, pale under their bronzed suntan. Wayne looked back at them over his shoulder as he started up the steps, and winked.

At exactly 2:20 p.m. they dropped Wayne Levitt through the trap door. At exactly 2:28 p.m., Tom Meek handed his limp body over to Jess and the other Texans. Kansas justice had been served.

XIV

It was their custom, so they buried Wayne Levitt as they had also buried young John Ewell Brown, in a smoothed-over grave without a marker of any kind. Jonathan even scattered ashes from his fire over the grave.

Jess had fetched back a bottle. He planted it near Jonathan's supper fire. When each man filled his tin cup with black java, he also liberally laced it with whiskey. Gabriel sat, cross-legged, like an Indian puzzling over the faint cadence and the majestically sweeping hands of his new watch. Potter looked over once, then gruffly said: "I'll teach you how to read the thing tomorrow on the trail."

They bedded down as usual and also awoke the following pre-dawn, as usual. Except that now there were only Jess, Jonathan, Gabe, Potter, and Harper. Five still going, two dead. Being short-handed would work a hardship, but they were men inured from birth to hardship, so they pushed the herd along, trading horses more often but otherwise giving no sign they were being overworked. As Harper said at the nooning, there wasn't much point in hiring a couple more hands, even if any such could be found in the little roundabout settlements, because the drive was nearly over.

After Prineville the next village was Douglas. Beyond that lay Liberty. Two days past Liberty lay other villages. They kept getting closer together. The land showed a farm here and there, occasional soddies where starved and faded people came out of the ground like digger squirrels to stare hungrily at all that meat going by, and finally they sighted a rider or two far out.

They made a camp at Six-Mile and let the cattle bed down on new grass. "It'll keep gettin' harder an' harder," said Harper Ellis, "for other herds to find this good graze. I reckon you could say, from a range rider's viewpoint, that's the only real advantage of bringin' up the first herd of the springtime."

Jonathan listened to them with growing impatience. He'd thought at least one of them would mention the village of Six-Mile, but none of them did.

Gabe said: "I camped in this identical spot six years back with the Chisums. Later in the spring, o' course. We got paid a visit by sod folks beggin' for a crippled or lame critter. It's a right mean life on folks livin' out here and wearin' themselves out tryin' to scratch a livin' out of a homesteaded section o' this prairie."

"Did Chisum give 'em a beef?" Jess asked, sopping up the gravy from his plate with a hard chunk of sourdough bread.

"He give it to 'em, Mistah Jess. He was a shrewd man, that John Chisum. He say . . . 'You don' feed 'em, they're desperate enough to shoot a critter, an' that'd be all right, too, 'ceptin' that it'd sure Lord stampede the herd and we'd lose maybe a hundred head.' Mistah John, for all his maybe bein' part Indian, was a mighty smart man."

Jonathan's impatience finally broke. He glared meanly at them. "Who's been to Six-Mile?" he shrilled. "Or are you all 'fraid of ridin' in for a little drink and maybe a game or two of cyards?"

Potter put his steady black gaze upon old Jonathan. "You're in no shape to ride over there," he said. "Here, fill up this cup again."

"Fill it up your ownse'f," snarled Jonathan, turning swiftly angry and vicious. "I'm in as fair a shape as any one of you. How come you fellers to always pick on me, anyway? Ever since we pulled out of Sweetwater. . . ."

"*Whoa*," said Jess, putting down his plate and gazing at Jonathan. "Where'd you build up so much bile? All Potter meant was. . . ."

"I know what he meant," stormed Jonathan, hooking himself up to both feet with the aid of the

180

wagon box. "I know damned well what the lot o' you mean, pityin' me an' lookin' down. . . ."

"Jonathan," broke in Harper Ellis, "I been to Six-Mile."

". . . You have?"

"Sure, old pardner, so sit back down and get rid of that big head of steam you're packin' around. It's not much of a place. Another Kansas prairie town. It's got several stores, about four saloons, some card rooms. I hit it one late afternoon a few years back when I took a jag of horses over to the Army remount depot with Ab Travis from San Antonio. We had us quite a time."

"Trouble?" Jonathan asked.

"No trouble at all, but then there was other Texans in town from a herd over on the eastern plain. We just about had the run of the place."

Jonathan blinked a bird-like look at Jess. "Still plenty early," he said. "We could lope in, have a few rounds, an' lope back."

Jess had known for some time this statement was coming. He didn't particularly want to take his crew into any of the Kansas towns until they got to rail's end at Wichita. After that everyone was on his own anyway. The trouble with hitting these lesser places was simply that they were not as tolerant or as varied in their offerings of entertainment as the big towns where drovers congregated by the hundreds. In a place like Six-Mile about all Texans could do was drink, maybe sit in a poker game, drink, perhaps flirt a little with saloon girls—and drink. It was the drinking that usually capped things. Nearly sixty days on the trail made a man lose a lot of his resistance.

"Well," demanded Jonathan, impaling Jess with his dry-hot stare. "We lope in, celebrate a mite, an' come right on back?"

Jess and Potter exchanged a look. Potter shrugged. Harper Ellis swallowed dryly; the idea was catching on with all of them. Gabe solemnly made quite a point of squinting at his watch— which he couldn't read. Jess stood up.

"All right. It won't do any good to tell you we got to be on the trail again come sunup. But we do. Jonathan, you want to ride in or drive the rig to the edge of town?"

"Ride!" exclaimed the *cocinero*. "Hot damn! Come on, you scalawags, shake a leg. Say, Harper, just how far is it over there?"

They were all arising now. "Not far," Harper answered. "You can see the lights yonder on the horizon. Maybe five miles, no more'n that."

They had branch water to wash by and slick down their hair. Hub grease was adequate for wiping over scuffed boots and every one of them had a clean butternut shirt. Beyond that they were content to beat dust out of their hats, reshape the crowns, then sidle over to Jess for a little advance, which was why he had that doeskin bag of money along—that, and emergencies. Each man drew $30.

They cut out fresh mounts, saddled up, and by that time even Jess was turning yeasty. It had been a long trail and an almighty dry one. They left camp with a whoop and a holler, loped the first six and a half miles straight toward the hull down light of Six-Mile, then slowed to a brisk trot because Jonathan, while he didn't make a sound, showed by his moonlighted face he was in pure agony.

Six-Mile lay near a chocolate-colored river that had scarcely any fall at all and therefore moved along like molten lead. It was dirty, sluggish, and smelled of rotting vegetation. They crossed it at a rocky ford and scarcely got their feet wet. Beyond, where the first buildings stood, there were shacks of crating covered with black waterproof paper that gave off a creosote stench when the sun was hot, and looked like cubes in the darkness.

Someone was banging on a piano at the upper end of town. Mostly the homes and shacks and stores were dark. Six-Mile's nightlife, like all frontier nightlife, didn't really get lively until after 10:00 p.m. It was working up to the point as Jess led them up through the southern part of town toward the glare of bright orange lamplight northward. Now and then a rider loped past. A few men stood in gloom along the boardwalks, talking and smoking. There were no women out at all and the hitch racks seemed nearly full up where the saloons were.

They tied up in front of a dry goods emporium,

stepped onto the plank walk, gave their shell belts a shift, and started forward. The fullness was leaving the overhead moon but the brightness was just about as sharp. It made Six-Mile look almost clean and wholesome.

The first saloon they entered was called the Sharpshooter. It was a popular place. Besides the townsmen in their little hats and elegant lavender sleeve garters, their sweat-shiny faces, and limp shirts of good broadcloth, there were a number of range men, booted and spurred and armed.

Jonathan led through the smoky crowd with his crab-like crippled gait arrow straight for the bar. The others followed, not so parched but just as unerring. No one paid them much heed; the room was crowded, full of tobacco smoke and noisy. The Kansas plains saw strangers come and go constantly. Texans were recognizable by their attire, and by their slow drawl, but from springtime on there were nearly as many Texans on the plains as Kansans. As long as there was no trouble, no one particularly heeded Texas men.

Jonathan slapped down a coin and bawled at the barkeep.

"Rye whiskey, pardner, and five glasses!"

Men gave way so the Texans could line up side-by-side.

Jonathan poured and drank and poured again and drank again. He dashed at the sting of quick tears; that whiskey was as green as grass.

A big man dressed as a cowboy looked around, saw black Gabriel at his side, and looked down his nose with an expression of veiled hostility. Gabe saw and ignored that look. The cowboy looked beyond Gabe. Potter Houston was looking straight at the cowboy with that dead-level malevolent black stare of his. The cowboy picked up his glass and walked away.

Jess and the others had their first drink fast, then nursed the second one. Not Jonathan. He'd had two before his friends got well set at the bar. He had his third while they were looking around the room. His fourth went down like red-hot fire and he paused to pant a little and wipe water from his eyes. The barman stepped over to put down Jonathan's change, saw four men watching him, and dropped the last large silver coin from his clenched fist, then went along. The night was young; he'd clip the Texans later.

There were some card games in progress. There were also several painted women circulating, keeping the men jolly and spending. One of them spied bronzed Jess and worked her way through the crowded press of bodies to him. She wasn't young any more and at one time she'd possessed a fragile type of pale beauty that was now just a shadow across her scarlet-lipped, weak face. But she had beautiful white teeth when she smiled up at him.

"Hello, Texas," she said. "I've been waiting for you since last fall. Where's your herd?"

"Out a few miles westerly," he answered. "Step up. I'll buy you a shot."

She squeezed in and caught the barman's harried eye. He brought her a glass already filled with colored sarsaparilla. "Four bits," he said. Jess handed him a coin and kept his palm open for the change. The barman handed it over along with a hard look. He'd *still* clip these Texans, but they'd have to get oiled first, and that tall, wise-eyed one might take a lot of oiling.

The girl turned and leaned with her elbows upon the bar top to gaze out over the room. "Good crowd tonight," she said absently. Jess agreed. Potter drifted past toward a poker game. Harper left the bar too, heading toward a faro layout. Gabe took what remained of their bottle and went with Jonathan over to a corner table; those two were here in Six-Mile for just one purpose and it wasn't poker or faro.

"You heading for Dodge City, Texas?"

Jess shook his head at her. "Wichita."

"You fellers got the first herd that's passed Six-Mile this spring."

"Yeah. We aim to have it that way, miss."

She studied Jess. At twenty-six he was a lot of man: tall, with his share of muscle packed inside a taut hide. Blue-eyed and sandy-haired. He had a quietness about him and a toughness.

"You're good-lookin'," she murmured, twisting from the waist. "Want another drink?"

They had another one; his costing a dime, hers still costing four bits. Then she switched from sarsaparilla to whiskey and he toyed with his third one, making it last, because the fumes were beginning to rise from behind his belt.

Over in their corner Gabe and Jonathan were steadily worrying that bottle to the bottom. Then Gabe slumped forward with his head across both arms and Jonathan had the last three fingers to triumph over all by himself. He did it, but only because he persevered. Then he tried to stand up. The table became in his dim consciousness something else, perhaps a boulder or a tree. He clutched it and gave one crippled leg a savage kick.

"Leggo," he growled, fiercely kicking again. "Leggo my leg, you danged Mexican. What you figure you're doin' anyway?" He lurched for the table with both hands and upset the empty bottle. At a nearby card game the players turned to look. Jonathan's voice rose to a snarl of wrath. "You thievin' varmints, leggo my legs or I'll salivate the pack of you. Haw! It's a damned Comanch'. I see him, the bloody devil!" Jonathan staggered half around, aimed a vicious kick, and let fly. His remaining sound leg skidded when the upraised one was still in mid-air. Suddenly he crashed down out of sight beyond the table. The card players roared. Other people turned to look. Old Jonathan was down on all fours, peering around the table, his hat gone, his eyes glassy, his lips curled into a savage expression. He was fumbling around with his right hand trying to find his .45. It had slipped around in front between his legs. One of the card players got up, stepped over, took away Jonathan's gun, and returned to his chair, still broadly grinning.

Jonathan gave up searching for his gun, aimed with one fist and mightily swung. "*Yow!*" he bellowed. "That'll hold the scalpin' varmint." He started lurching around as though to strike another of those invisible enemies. People moved in to form a ring. They roared and pointed and encouraged the *cocinero*. Jonathan made a fierce lunge and locked his arms around an imagined throat. He sat there, gritting his teeth and straining to strangle his foeman.

The girl with Jess said: "Didn't he come in here with you, Texas?"

Jess didn't answer. Potter came strolling over with a wry expression. Harper, too, was pushing through. Potter said, looking at Jonathan: "Maybe we'd best head on back, Jess. He's goin' to be like a wildcat to hold on his damned horse. You had enough?"

Jess said he had. The three of them went forward, pushed through, and grabbed old Jonathan, who immediately and furiously lashed out at them.

"Halp!" he squawked as Potter lifted him. "Halp! The red devils got me." He kicked and scratched, swung wild punches and arched his body. Potter motioned for Harper to grab an arm. "Halp! God 'n' liberty, remember the Alamo. Come on you Texas boys, we'll scalp the passel of 'em!"

Someone held the door open for them to carry their spitting, howling, rumpled companion out into the cool night air. Everyone uproariously howled with glee as old Jonathan knocked off Potter's hat and tried to bite Harper's restraining hand. Then they got him outside. Jess went back for Gabe, who couldn't quite command his legs to work, so Jess had almost to carry him out, too. But first he retrieved Jonathan's gun.

In the view of Texas trail riders it had been a very successful night. Very successful, indeed.

XV

They broke camp the following morning after sunup. Well after sunup. Jess had cooked breakfast; he wasn't very good at it. Gabe ran behind the wagon at the smell of frying salt beef. Jonathan, they propped upon his wagon seat, hitched his team, and stuffed the lines into his clammy fingers. He was as gray as warmed-over death, his eyes trickled, and he said nothing to any of them.

Fortunately the trail was good until high noon when some riders came out, six of them, to buy a few head of beef, which Jess declined to sell them because with only him and Potter and Harper to cut them out and attempt to drive them away from the rest of the herd a stampede might ensue. The Kansans left grumblingly. A mile beyond the herd hit broken country.

Gabriel was sufficiently recovered by noon to pull his hat brim low over aching, bloodshot eyes, and to keep the drag moving. Jonathan drooped along in the trail dust, still more dead than alive. He stopped twice to lean far out over the side of his wagon. When it got good and hot, he drank some water, which he didn't retain very long, but afterward he seemed to perk up a little.

The herd, fortunately, followed wide established trails that threaded the broken country. Still, Jess and Potter and Harper had their work cut out for them; hard, hot, dehydrating work for the long-horns were turning tender-footed. It always happened near the end of the trail. At that, though, the iron-hoofed cattle of Texas walked three times as far as any other kind of critters could travel before turning leg-weary and tender. There was one advantage to this; if they stampeded, they wouldn't run far before slowing to a gimpy walk.

Sundown caught them halfway across the broken plain. Jess had Jonathan hunt water and set up camp. He and the others kept pushing the long-horns until just short of dark, trying to get clear of the breaks before nightfall; it would save a lot of hunting through little twisted cañons come daylight, if they could push the herd beyond, out where flat prairie began again. They didn't quite make it, though, which meant they'd get to sleep in the following day because they couldn't begin to make their gather without daylight to see by.

Jonathan had the stew cooking, the coffee aromatically bubbling, their blanket rolls flung down, when they rode wearily in and silently got down to rig up their rope holding corral, stumbling around in the dark to accomplish this.

Gabe ate sparingly. The others ate like horses. Old Jonathan avoided their accusing glances and kept to himself at the fireside, from time to time muttering some imprecation to himself under his breath. He was always very touchy after one of his monumental drunks; the others knew it and generally they left him alone. Gabe wasn't so touchy but they were tired; there was no sly banter that night.

Six-Mile was far behind. Like Prineville, it was already beginning to lose its vividness. It wouldn't be entirely forgotten, but, as fresh events crowded their lives, it would retreat farther and farther into memory.

The following dawn they were all up and stirring, although there was no hurry, for daylight wouldn't come for another long hour. Jonathan was still a little shaky, so was Gabe, but at least they both took hold as they had before, which released Jess from the cooking, an event Potter frankly and audibly welcomed.

"You are a good trail boss," he said, half smiling

as they squatted to eat. "But Lord deliver me from a drive you do the cookin' for."

Jess eyed Gabe, and then Jonathan. They averted their faces. Chagrin had set in with both of them. Harper smacked his lips over their fried sourdough bread soaked in beef grease, washed down with acid-like black coffee.

"Dependable men," he said. "That's what a feller needs on the trail. Hard-workin', industrious . . . sober . . . dependable men."

Jonathan gave him a venomous look and snarled under his breath. They had their morning smoke sitting on the ground for a change, instead of sitting their saddles awaiting sunlight. Gabe said: "No more. I never goin' to do that again."

Harper threw back his head and roared. Potter broadly smiled. Jess twinkled a merry look at Gabriel. "I've heard that same promise a thousand times before," he said. "And it usually lasts from about Six-Mile to Wichita. Gabe, there's no such thing as never. I learned that ten years ago."

"Oh," crooned Harper, "*you* weren't so bad, Gabe. *You* just went to sleep on the table until Jess packed you outside. It was Jonathan. Hell's handles, he was down on all fours with everyone in Six-Mile standin' there howling, fightin' half the Mexican raiders this side of the Río Grande, then polishin' off a whole herd of Comanche warriors. It was quite a fight."

Jonathan sprang up, flung coffee over their fire,

192

stamped to the wagon, and hurled the coffee pot inside. He stamped back and began furiously loading up their other camp effects. His face was as black as thunder but he never said a word. Jess watched a moment, grinning, then jerked his head at the others. Sunup was breaking, off in the hazy east. It was time to be rigging out and riding.

They got up into the breaks with soft daylight stabbing downward into the shallow cañons. By the time they got the drag end of the herd moving northward again, it was broad daylight. At noon they were across the broken country and out onto the northward prairie again. The herd was strung out for miles, a thousand longhorned, orry-eyed, peanut-brained, slab-sided, vicious-tempered Texas cattle that raised up a dust visible for fifteen miles, shuffling along behind a big buckskin lead steer that seemed to have no purpose in life but to keep everlastingly walking northward. His ears flopped, his horns glistened, his gait was dignified, and his expression was detached. In every drive there was one exactly like him; the men talked to him as an equal, they wrote songs about him, and, when they saw him walk into the last corral at rail's end, they were saddened for him.

For two days nothing happened. The weather held warm and clear, the grass was more than adequate, there were places for the herd to tank up on clean water—which was not clean after they trampled on across it—and, although there were increasing signs of civilization, the miles ticked off steadily.

"Wichita," crowed Harper Ellis that second night, "the jewel of the Longhorn Trail. Someday I'll buy me a rockin' chair, haul it out onto the prairie each summer, an' sit an' rock, and throw stones when the herds go by, with me sleepin' on real cotton every night and eatin' woman-cooked grub, while dumb damned Texas men push beef up for me to carve into."

"Mistah Ha'per," drawled Gabriel, eyeing Harper's big hooked nose and other features equally as ugly. "Where you goin' to find this here woman?"

Jonathan squealed with delight. Potter laughed and Harper turned gravely to consider his tormentor. "Gabriel," he solemnly responded, "how soon you want to commence blowin' that horn?" The threat rolled off Gabe like water off a duck's back. The others grinned, and Gabe grinned back.

"Well, anyway," Harper said, "this face saves me a heap of money. Back there in Six-Mile that little painted heifer didn't shine up an' talk me into buyin' her no sarsaparilla. That was Jess she cuddled up to."

The joshing went on until bedtime. Next morning at breakfast it started up again, but the jibes were directed toward Jonathan. Because he had a thin skin, he was still smarting when the four horsemen loped out to get the herd on its feet and

194

strung out. They covered four miles without a halt, then Gabe, who was heading up the lead, loped back to inform Jess there was a party of horsemen across their onward path.

"Range men?" Jess asked. "If so, I reckon they'll be wantin' to keep our herd clear of theirs."

"I didn't see no drive, Mistah Jess. Jus' them saddle backers sitting up there, watchin' us."

Jess turned a fresh look at Gabe, and kept looking. He didn't open his mouth. Gabe crinkled his forehead and faintly nodded. This silent communication reinforced Gabe's last words—and the quiet way he'd said them. Rustlers.

Kansas had its share of them; sometimes they were called sooners because they'd sooner steal a few head off passing herds, then hire out to work as range riders. They never stole more than perhaps forty or fifty head—unless a drive looked short-handed, then they might risk running off more, relying on that short-handedness to prevent pursuit. Usually, like every variety of human vulture, they were cowardly, stole just enough to irritate owners but never enough to warrant a layover while owners and drovers tracked them down.

Sooners were the bane of the Longhorn Trail. Not as deadly as Indians or as vicious as Comancheros, but, because they cropped up perennially in ever increasing numbers, more costly than both together.

"Go tell Potter and Harper," said Jess. "And

Gabe, stay up on the wings. I'll take the point from here on."

It was a long ride up the far side of the herd. Longhorns practically ignored horsebackers as long as the riders didn't get too close or didn't slide in behind them, then suddenly appear. Still and all, for Jess to go from the drag up to the point where the buckskin steer paced quietly along took almost a full hour because the cattle were strung out for miles. When he got up there, he saw no one, no horsemen, no settlement folks, not hide or hair of anyone at all.

He knew Gabe far too well to discount what he'd been told, so he made another big sashay eastward, then westward, searching for riders. He found them westward. They were easing down over a small swale, dropping from sight over in the west. It made him suspicious, so he scouted them still more and got the count as they angled along out of sight of the plodding cattle. Six of them, each man well mounted and well armed. Sooners as sure as Jess was a foot tall.

He dropped back carefully to the point and rode it for an hour, then drifted down the far, or westerly, side of the drive until he found Gabe and Potter. He told them what he'd seen and what he suspected.

Potter was sanguine. "It's about time," he said. "Things've been goin' far too good." He wiped off sweat, replaced his hat, and patted the upended steel butt plate of his booted Winchester. "Well," he said to Jess, raising both brows, "it's hit them first or they'll hustle a few head after we go into camp. That's how they operate. Wait until drovers are in camp, then rustle off the far upper end of the herd."

Jess nodded. "I'll ride around and tell Harper. Gabe, take the point again and poke along like you don't suspect a thing. Potter, drift back and tell Jonathan we'll make camp ahead of sundown. Tell him to stop wherever there's water."

They split up. Over in the west, where those ghostly riders had disappeared, there wasn't a sign of them. When Jess located Harper through the burning dust and told him, Ellis was pleased. In a dust-dry voice he croaked out a resounding blasphemy and concluded with a grisly promise. "Anything beats doin' nothin' but eatin' longhorn dust," he said. "What's the plan?"

Jess told him. They'd camp early, then stalk the rustlers. With any luck at all they should locate them before they reached the herd. After that, kill as many as they could. A very elementary plan for very elementary men.

Jess was holding his horse to a snail's pace to let the plodding longhorns drift on past when he saw Jonathan veer off and head for a place where several cottonwoods stood. He was satisfied. A skyward glance told him there was about another hour and a half of daylight. He slowed his horse still more, the drag went plodding past   tender-footed, most of it—then he angled on over where Jonathan was dumping out blanket rolls and hobbling about the routine business of setting up camp. He told Jonathan what the plan was and got a grim nod.

"I reckon you'll want me to stay here 'n' mind the damned camp," said Jonathan. "All right. But there was a time when fellers was right relieved to have me along on a skulkin' mission."

Jess said nothing. Arguments never prevailed against Jonathan's iron-headed stubbornness anyway; it was better to let him think what he wished, so long as he did what Jess wished him to do.

Potter was the next one to arrive at the new camp. He simply nodded and off-saddled, tied his horse until Harper came in, then those two set up the rope corral and put the horses inside. It was never much of a chore; after a month of the same daily and nightly routine, the saddle stock knew what to expect and was usually complacent about it.

The last one in was Gabe. As he headed for the spring to wash, he called over his shoulder: "Seen one of 'em watchin' the leaders from a long way off northwesterly. He sure looked to be ridin' a fine big chestnut horse."

Jess joined Gabe at the water hole. They used the same lye soap and the same grimy old towel. Potter and Harper brought over their own towel and soap. As the four of them knelt, washing off dust and sweat, Potter said: "Be a hell of a note to pot-shoot us a mess of homesteaders who're only tryin' to steal a head or two for feedin' their women and kids."

"We'll be sure enough," said Jess who'd attacked sooners before. "Their breed doesn't just take one or two head."

Gabe finished and sat back in cottonwood shade with his collar still rolled under and his hair wet. He made a smoke, inhaled, tilted his head, and exhaled. This was the pleasantest time of day and washing off strong-smelling trail dust was one of the truly rewarding, refreshing parts of closing daylight.

"Boys," he said softly, watching the others from his comfortable place, "why is it, with all the infernal torments Nature sends against us, human beings got to go around plaguin' one another?"

Potter looked around. "Because, as you just said, Gabe . . . they're human beings. No more treacherous, mean, dishonest, lyin' animal on God's green earth. Come on, let's get back and eat a bait of Jonathan's stew, then go prove how ornery humans are by killin' us some sooners."

The sun was dropping low; the sky was turning red. It was breathless and hot even yet, as they plodded back to eat an early supper.

XVI

Kansas rustlers normally had one great disadvantage. The land was flat; they could be seen miles going and coming. These sooners, though, had an added disadvantage, which had to do with the way they struck a herd—always far ahead. Of course, providing the drovers were not suspicious, this invariably proved lucrative, but if they happened, as with Jess's crew, to suspect skullduggery was afoot, there was every reason to believe they'd resist the sooners, attack, in which case, if the Texans used only moderate slyness, they could catch the rustlers at work.

Still, the thieves were successful often enough to keep them at their trade. In fact, as the drives grew larger and closer together, they increased alarmingly. And, as with Jess's herd, when they spied out a drive, found it to be short-handed, they could be almost automatically relied upon to attack it.

The sooners were very often local homesteaders who'd formed into raiding bands after their farming and ranching efforts had left them on the verge of deprivation and want. Initially they'd raided only for meat, but of course the enterprising among them very soon recognized the opportunities for a greater gain, thus the rustler crew came into existence. Or as Potter Houston said as the Texans were saddling up in the descending gloom:

"Pretty hard for a hungry man, once his gut is filled, not to think of what he needs next, which is a little money. It's only a whoop an' a holler from a big plate of rustled meat to a poke full of gold for a few head run off when no one's lookin'."

"On'y this time," put in Gabe, "somebody goin' to *be* lookin'."

They left camp heading northwesterly into the dying day's red haze. They had fresh animals, full bellies, all their armament and plenty of ammunition. The only other thing required was resolve, and, if they hadn't possessed that from birth, they'd never have been this far from Texas anyway.

The critters were still grazing so they had to thread their way carefully in order not to start a panic. But it had been one of those dehydrating days; the longhorns were as tired as were the Texans. They would raise a bulging eye here and there, or drop their long faces and threateningly shake their horns, but otherwise they kept a wary eye on the riders and went on grazing.

Jess was leading his crew by memory only; it was too difficult in the day's ending to make out distant landmarks. It was a trifle early for the rustlers to be at work. They ordinarily awaited full darkness. The night was warm, almost hot; there was a feeling of electricity in the air. Gabe sniffed and looked solemn. Harper raised his big hooked nose, too, then he and Gabe exchanged a meaningful look. It felt like storm weather: hot, utterly still, almost breathless, and charged with static electricity that made horses' manes and tails splay out.

Potter interpreted that look. "All we need," he growled. "Just one more stampede."

Jess said nothing. They were approaching the area between the herd and the western gully where he'd last seen those shadowy riders. Once, he swung down and listened, but there was nothing, so he led them on a little distance farther before making his final halt. That time they picked up sound from the earth.

"Riders comin'," Jess stated, "but they're a piece northward."

"Better go afoot," cautioned Potter, but Jess shook his head, mounted up, and signaled for the others to do the same. He obviously had no wish at all to be involved in a gunfight with the rustlers in a place where some fluke of Nature might bring a thousand stampeding longhorns over the top of him as had happened with young Jeb.

They rode softly, though. Jess's wish was fairly clear. If he could continue on his present course and slide between the sooners and the herd, he'd have the night riders cut off so that, whether they fought back or not, they'd have to withdraw westerly, which was away from the herd. The important thing were his longhorns, much more important than catching six scruffy rustlers.

Gabe hissed and halted. Instantly the others also drew rein. Gabe pointed rigidly to his left, which was westward. For a moment there was nothing, then somewhere off in the rusty dusk a solitary horseman passed over rock and made a noise doing so. At once Harper Ellis dropped down the far side of his horse with a Winchester in his hands. The others were a little slower doing the same thing. Jess gestured for them to spread out. There was no time to wonder aloud over a solitary rustler off by himself, unless of course he'd been detached and sent southward to make certain, as his cronies worked, some circling night hawk from the Texas camp didn't accidentally come along and spoil things.

Jess took his horse over to Potter, handed the swarthy man its reins, then started straight ahead out through the night toward those sounds of a rider. When he was beyond sight of his men, Jess made a close analysis of the oncoming man's route, then dropped to the ground in the grass where he'd pass. It was an old Indian trick.

The rider came up. He was slouched in the saddle but alert. He was looking off southwesterly in the direction of Jonathan's camp. Fortunately for someone, he hadn't tugged forth his carbine to ride with it ready across his lap as was the custom.

Jess rose up as the man passed ten feet ahead. "Hold it," he softly called. "Haul up, pardner, and don't make a move or a sound."

The rustler was dumbfounded. He halted, stiffened in his saddle, and started to look back, caught himself, and froze. Jess moved over behind the horse's rump. He ordered the man to drop his armament. This was done without argument. Jess then directed his prisoner to keep right on riding at a slow walk. As the horse obediently moved out, Jess walked along behind it, herding both man and animal right up to where Gabe and Harper and Potter Houston closed in, converging.

Potter hauled their captive from his saddle, roughly frisked him for more weapons, found none, and spun the Kansan around for Jess to have his first good look. The rustler was a youth no more than eighteen years old.

Jess eyed the ashen lips and unnaturally dark eyes. The Kansan was badly frightened; whether he'd made many raids or not—and at his age it seemed unlikely—he seemed to know what Texans usually did with sooners. They usually set up their camp wagon's tongue, lashed it back, and hanged them, buried them quietly, and went on, leaving an unmarked grave.

Jess said: "Where are your friends?"

The youth painfully swallowed and said nothing.

Harper Ellis stepped over, bent from the waist, and shoved his ugly, bronzed face close. "Got a Bowie knife in my boot," he murmured. "It's near a foot long an' sharp enough to split a hair. Sooner, you ever see a man walkin' off carryin' half his entrails inside his hat? No? Well, then, where are your friends?"

The ashen-faced youth raised a hand and gestured vaguely with it. "In a draw, waitin' for me to come back an' tell 'em the coast's clear."

Harper straightened up slightly. "Then they was fixin' to run off a few."

"Yes, sir. But only because we need the meat."

"Sure," murmured Harper. "Sure, boy. Fifty, sixty head. That's a heap of meat, Kansas. Your pappy amongst 'em? He teach you to be a dirty thief?"

"He's dead. Died last winter of the complaint. I got only my maw and three little sisters."

Harper gazed for a time at the boy, then turned toward Jess. Even in the gloom Harper's face showed no stomach for hanging this one whether his story was true or not—and it probably was because it was the common story on the Kansas plains—he was a little young for lynching.

Jess said: "Boy, you take us to the others where the camp is. Then you can go."

The lad's dark and stricken gaze fastened itself upon Jess. "I can't do that, mister," he whispered. "You're goin' to kill them. I'm no Judas."

Potter, who'd been silent up to now, paced across where Jess was, whispered something to him, and walked over to take the rustler's horse and gaze back. Jess nodded, so Potter made a peremptory gesture for the youth to mount up, which he did.

Potter also got astride. So did Jess and Gabe and Harper Ellis. Without asking a question the others rode along with Potter, who led the rustler's horse on a very loose lead shank. They passed along a hundred yards before it dawned on Gabe and Harper—and their prisoner—what Potter was doing. He was allowing the rustler's horse plenty of slack and the horse was heading back the way he'd come. All the Texans had to do was keep up.

The youth moved to touch his reins. Potter's baleful black stare stopped him. A while farther along he tried to ease his weight to the off side so the horse would respond. That time Potter leaned far over and tapped his arm.

"Son, you're never goin' to see your mammy or your sisters actin' like this, an' let me pass on t' you something else. You're a sight more valuable to them alive and maybe hungry, than dead, which you're likely to be the next time you join up with the sooners."

The youth went along after that, stone-faced and resigned. His horse plodded back over its earlier trail innocently betraying its rider's friends. The last scarlet shadows turned somber black and the whittled-down moon cast weak, ghostly light downward.

They went almost two miles before Gabe hissed as he'd done before, bringing them all to a halt. Whatever it was that had caught his attention was withheld from the others when their captive straightened in his saddle sucking in a quick, sharp breath. He was cut down from behind by Harper Ellis with a fierce slash over the head by a Winchester barrel before he could make the yell of warning. He fell like a lump and lay still between his horse and the horse of Potter Houston. For a moment the Texans gazed downward, then Gabe said: "Dead campfire. Sniff up high an' you'll pick up the scent."

They smelled it and they dismounted. Jess handed his reins to Gabe. So did the others. Gabe's dark face was expressionless. Whether he liked being delegated as horse holder or not didn't matter now; they were too near, and time was running out for them. There was no time for arguing.

Jess whispered: "Take 'em southward, Gabe, and for gosh sakes hang onto them no matter what happens."

Gabriel silently turned and started walking. The others came close to whisper briefly, then Jess led off due west following the strongest scent of that doused fire. The land was uneven out here. There were erosion gullies and tufts of forage grass that grew to a height of twelve inches, just high enough to trip a man unless he watched closely to avoid them. Up ahead a horse blew through its nose. Another horse shuffled shod hoofs as though tethered to something and impatient to be moving.

They dropped down and skylined the onward flow of land. In some ways their impending attack paralleled the course they'd successfully used back at the Comanchero camp. But these Kansas cow thieves were now nearly as wily and alert as those other renegades had been. One of them was squatting on the ground, smoking a cigarette that alternately glowed when he drew on it, and paled out when he did not.

Harper Ellis was slightly to Jess Howard's right. There wasn't much tall grass over there. Slightly behind Jess was Potter Houston, leaning upon his grounded carbine and solemnly eyeing the rustler camp.

There were five saddled horses up there, clearly visible against the skyline. There were also five men, two of them squatting near the smoking ring where their fire had been, three of them standing over by the horses. One of the men by the horses said something, low and indistinguishable, to the squatting men, who arose and stood a moment, then began to turn. One of them stopped and turned back. He was peering straight out in the direction of Harper Ellis.

"Wait a minute!" he called to the others. "That damned kid's out there." He had spotted Harper. Potter Houston at once shifted position, planted one knee upon the ground, and raised his carbine. Jess did the same.

"Naw," growled someone over by the horses. "The kid couldn't be back yet. We'll make a little sashay down where he is, though, and get his report."

"I tell you," insisted that rustler, squinting out where he could distinguish Harper Ellis's lanky, kneeling frame when Potter fired.

The rustler flung out his arms and crumpled with a harsh cry. Jess also fired. The man nearest the first casualty was spun like a top before he also fell.

XVII

The other three went for their guns at the same time they hurled themselves to the ground. Harper Ellis poured a low fire toward those men, but if it scored, no one knew it then. After that initial, slashing attack, the Texans had to separate and stay apart because the rustlers were fiercely firing. One of them would shout after each shot. Jess tried to get that one, but the man never seemed to roll in the same direction twice.

One of the tethered horses broke loose in panic and ran southward. The other two animals tugged, but as the fight turned sporadic and its combatants moved swiftly away from that spot where two of their companions had gone down within seconds of each other, the animals were less involved.

Jess dropped back. He moved left and right, then forward again. He was confident of the outcome since the odds were better than even now, but he also thought those desperate outlaws would sooner or later try to get back to their horses. He intended to be handy with his weapons when they did.

The fight devolved into a nocturnal duel between men who could not see each other and had only muzzle blasts to aim at. Then, after a half hour of this fruitless kind of fighting, there was a long lull.

Jess thought the Kansans were coming together out there somewhere in the darkness. He could imagine what they'd say to one another—get to saddle and break it off before the drovers killed them all. He lay there in the grass as close as he dared get, concentrating his whole attention upon the horses. Potter Houston crawled up and also lay belly down. Potter said nothing but he'd obviously come to the same conclusion as Jess.

But the minutes dragged by and no one appeared over there. They had an excellent sighting of the horses; if a man had crawled up to them, even though the animals knew his scent, they'd still look at him, and that was what Potter and Jess kept watching for. A horse to snort softly and look down into the surrounding grass.

A man suddenly called forth, his voice honed to a hard sharpness by his peril. "Hey, you Texans! We had enough. You drop back an' let us ride off, and we won't bother your herd."

Jess answered: "I got a better idea, Kansas. You 'n' your friends stand up unarmed and reach for the sky."

"No, by God," the sharp voice answered swiftly. "There'll be no lynchin'."

"I didn't say anything about a hangin'," stated Jess. "All we want is to haul you into some town an' let your own law handle you."

The Kansan's answer, as before, shot right back. "Amounts to the same thing, Texas. The law'd likely set us to swingin', too." He hesitated briefly, then said: "Call it off an' we'll head on out. We ain't hurt you none anyhow."

"Not because you wouldn't have if you'd got the chance," growled Potter. "Leavin' a pack like you on the loose is like puttin' a wolf in a henhouse." Potter fired toward the sound of that rustler's voice, and at once the fight turned brisk again.

Jess had to roll when Potter fired because the rustlers fired at Houston's gun flash. He and Potter became separated again. Harper Ellis, northward and slightly ahead of his friends, let fly three fast shots as rapidly as he could lever and tug the trigger. Someone over where the rustlers were retreating cried out, then fell to moaning. Harper had scored a hit.

Potter and Jess shot their Winchesters dry and turned to their .45s. They permitted the rustlers no rest, raking the night left and right with bullets. For a little while the return fire was disorganized and ragged. Eventually it stopped altogether. The Texans kept firing. A man yelled from out of the westerly darkness that he was surrendering, that he would come forward unarmed if the Texans would agree to hold off shooting.

Silence descended again, deep and ominous. By Jess's count there had to still be two of them out there. He called to the surrendering man. "You'd better not try it alone, mister. If it's a trick, you're going to get cut in two."

"It's no trick!" yelled the Kansan. "I'm all that's left." He waited a moment, then repeated his offer to come forward unarmed. Jess called first to Potter and Harper, warning them, then he ordered the rustler to walk out where they could see him.

He did. His silhouette appeared through the solid night with weak star shine revealing that he was almost a full half mile southward of those tethered horses. Potter was down there across from him. As the outlaw shuffled ahead, Potter rose up off the ground to parallel him with a cocked .45 trained upon the man.

Harper Ellis waited. When he saw Jess also stand up and cover the prisoner, Harper finally walked on down to join the other two.

The Kansan was a man in his fifties, grizzled and close-eyed and unkempt. He was tall and thin with a gamy odor to him that was compounded of man sweat, horse sweat, and many smoky campfires. He halted where he had a good sighting of the three Texans, slowly swung his head, and finally said: "Where's the rest of 'em?"

Potter moved over to relieve the man of a boot knife and a Derringer; otherwise, the rustler was unarmed. "There aren't but the three of us," Potter said, shoving the man over in front of Jess. "Say the word, Jess. I'll use his own damned hide-out gun on him."

Jess shook his head. "He's got some graves to dig first," he said, then addressed their captive. "How many of you were there?"

"Six," replied the man truthfully. "Five men an' a cussed kid."

"We got the kid over by the herd. Are you plumb sure the others stopped lead?"

"Mister, I ought to be," dryly responded the outlaw. "I was over there with 'em. Them damned slugs was comin' thicker'n a swarm of bees. I'll show you where they went down."

Jess shook his head. He still was not certain. "In the morning," he told the outlaw. "When we come back up here with our wagon and tools for them burials." He looked at Harper and Potter. "What about the kid?" he asked.

Potter had the first answer. "Leave him. When he comes to, he'll find the bodies. If that doesn't scare the whey outen him from ever tryin' this again, I'll be right surprised."

Harper agreed, then slung his Winchester over a bent arm, saying he'd go after Gabe and their horses. He walked off.

Jess and Potter, keeping their captive in front, went over to where the outlaws' horses were tied, removed the bridles of all but one horse, slapped the horses, and watched them race away. "Goin' to he some wailing when those animals arrive back home," Potter observed.

They talked to their captive. His name, he told them, was Jack Pruett; the men with him had been, like he was, homesteaders who'd starved out on their dry land claims. He named them all and said they'd done well rustling a few head the year before, so had organized into a crew to make it really pay. Then he told them something they thought a good deal about in the ensuing hours.

"You turn me over to the law an' maybe I won't get much. It depends on where you turn me in. Around here the folks is sympathetic to us sooners. Any jury'd turn us loose. The local folks got no call to love you Texas fellers."

Jess said: "How about up at Wichita?"

Pruett's candor was less certain about that. "No, too many danged outlanders get on the juries up there, mister. They got a different view of things, especially rustlin' or horse stealin'."

By the time Gabe returned with Harper and their mounts, Jess and Potter had sized up their prisoner. Pruett was a hatchet-faced, sly-eyed man, but he was not a liar. That he'd been an outlaw before becoming a sooner they did not doubt, although he refused to deny or confirm this when they asked more questions. They set him upon his own horse, got astride their animals, and rode off. When they came to the spot where they'd left the youth, he was gone and so was his horse. They then struck out for their camp, and, when they rode in, Jonathan was waiting, shotgun in hand, creased and seamed coppery face twisted with anxiety and curiosity.

They tied their prisoner to a wagon wheel, cleaned and re-loaded their weapons, then drank coffee, and had a final smoke. It had been another long day; the moon was fading far down the purple night, and, if they got any rest at all, it wouldn't be very much before it was time to roll out again.

They bedded down, leaving the captive tied. He could sleep if he cared to, or if he could; they were cold toward him and callous.

When Jonathan came shuffling around to poke up his breakfast fire a few hours later, the prisoner asked him for a drink of water. Jonathan tossed the man a canteen and turned his back on him. Jonathan had participated in many a well-deserved prairie hanging; he viewed Jack Pruett as a prime target for the same rough kind of justice. Still, when the others came around to squat and eat, Jonathan took a plate and cup over to Pruett. It was, in the Texas view, one thing to mete out prairie justice, swift and final, and quite another to be needlessly cruel.

They loaded the wagon, then Potter took Pruett and a shovel back where the fight had taken place. Jess, Gabe, and Harper Ellis got the herd to its feet and started northward again. They couldn't make much time, but they didn't particularly care about that as long as Potter converged on them some-where up ahead.

He did, when the sun was a fiery disc almost directly overhead and Jonathan was cursing over having to make another waterless nooning. He and Pruett rode in drenched with sweat, Pruett badly used up after digging four deep graves and re-covering them.

"Smoothed 'em over," reported Potter, stepping into the shade of the texas. "Unless Pruett here tells what happened, no one's going to find those graves."

They fed the prisoner. He was by this time thor-oughly demoralized, wrung out and wilted. He scarcely ate at all, but he consumed an inordinate amount of water, and sat there in the shade, looking more disreputable and defeated than ever.

As Potter moved around by the tailgate to stow the shovel Pruett had used at his grisly task, he beckoned to Jess with his head. When they were apart from the others, he said in a low, gruff voice: "Set him loose, Jess. The main thing is that he's not going to say anything about what happened. He's plenty scairt."

Jess nodded. He had good reason for not wish-ing to hand Pruett over to Kansas law; it had happened before, and it could happen again. Kansas law took a dim view of Texans shooting it out with renegades or anyone else up in Kansas Territory. And where there was a survivor—which most drovers made a particular point to see that there was *not* so only one version of such meetings was given—Kansas law had more than once turned upon Texans.

He and Potter returned to the others. Jonathan was already striking camp. Gabe and Harper were helping him. No one paid the slightest attention to the unwanted prisoner. He sat there, free to move, his empty hip holster hanging lightly at his side, his sweat-drenched shirt clinging to a scrawny, wiry chest and arms. When Jess and Potter halted to gaze downward, Pruett looked up at them. For several seconds no one said a word, then Pruett painfully swallowed.

"Listen, boys," he mumbled. "I been straight with you. I ain't no liar an' I never was. I been a lot o' things but not a liar. Never had no use for liars. Listen, I won't say a thing. You set me loose an' I give you m' word I won't say a thing."

"Sure not," stated Jess. "It'd likely be your neck as well as ours if you did. That's not what's bothering me, Pruett. What's to keep you from gettin' up another band an' settin' up in business again?"

"No, mister. No chance o' that around here no more. You laid low the only two fellers hereabouts who'd ride as sooners last night. The rest of us was just sort of volunteers, taggin' along. No, Mister Range Boss, you done broke the back of the sooner camp in these parts. I give you my word for that."

Jess said: "Get up, Pruett. Get on your horse. You can go. But you'd better hope we never meet again. I aim to remember you."

Jonathan, Gabe, and Harper strolled around to watch the enormously relieved outlaw walk to his horse, mount up, cast them one rearward look, then hook his horse hard and go spurring away as though he expected a bullet in the back.

Jonathan snorted disdainfully. "He's sure a trustin' soul, ain't he? Well, let's get t' rollin'. We're low on water, got to find a creek or something to make night camp by, otherwise you fellers are goin' to be spittin' cotton."

They wordlessly went after their mounts, wordlessly mounted, and headed for the drifting herd. Less than eight hours before they'd been solely concerned with killing men and keeping others from killing them. Now their primary concern was water. They'd find it; particularly in Kansas in the springtime, they all knew they'd find it. All they had to do was keep the herd moving in the right direction, and that proved no difficulty at all because, whatever else they and their kind uncharitably said of longhorn cattle, the Texas critters had a nose for sniffing out water. They paced along, sniffing, turning their wicked-horned heads left and right to catch the scent of water, and eventually, as sundown drew close, they picked up the smell, quickened their gait, came to a sluggish, low-banked river, and waded in to fill up blissfully.

Afterward, the critters were perfectly content to chew their cuds and bed down.

That electricity that had been in the air the day before was no longer discernible. If there had been a brewing storm, the wind had shifted sufficiently to take it somewhere else. Jonathan made his wet camp and hummed at his work. All was well, and the trail was nearing its end.

XVIII

Ordinarily longhorn herds arriving in the vicinity of Wichita sought a quiet piece of prairie and encamped there while the range boss drifted on into town in search of a buyer.

This process was almost reversed when Jess Howard's drive appeared, low and strung out over the low horizon, a thousand head dwarfed by the high sky and the endless land to ant size, but plainly visible to the folks in Wichita. Jess was still an hour or two from loping on ahead to search for the campsite when two riders came dusting it out from town, one of them wearing a coat with split tails that flapped out behind his saddle, the other one more at home in the saddle, lanky and competent-looking, and smoking a long, slightly bent cigar.

Potter intercepted those two as he and Gabe converged on the point position to ease the lead steer off westerly, away from any possible inadvertent meeting with strangers that might frighten the cattle.

The man with the Prince Albert coat was short, burly as a bear, gray-headed, and sharp-eyed. He asked if Potter was the trail boss and, finding that he was not, went flapping on down the line with Potter to locate Jess. Gabe was left alone up in the point position, but he knew very well what had to be done, and he did it. He veered the herd off westerly where new grass grew fetlock high and an azure sky speckled with far clouds dropped pale shadows over the prairie.

Jess was coming around the east side of the herd when he saw Potter and the strangers coming. He halted to wait.

As Potter pulled down, he gestured to the burly man in the coat. "This here is Abner Fowler, Jess. This other gent is his cow boss, Charles Spires." Potter introduced Jess to the strangers and dropped back. Spires broadly grinned; he was a big, hard-eyed individual, armed, and perfectly at home under the present condition. He and Jess shook hands.

"Been quite a spell," said the cow boss. "Last spring about six, seven weeks later'n this, wasn't it?"

Jess smiled. "You don't look much different, Charley," he said, "for all your livin' up here with the Yankees."

Spires chuckled. "They got the money, Jess."

Abner Fowler cleared his throat. He was patently an impatient man. "How many head, Mister Howard?" he asked briskly, grunting around in the saddle to size up the nearest animals. "A thousand less maybe half a hundred, more or less. You a buyer, Mister Fowler?"

"I am, sir. I am. What price you got on 'em?"

Jess was briefly silent, gazing at Fowler's shrewd eyes and lipless gash of a mouth. "I can't buy 'em an' sell 'em, too," he countered. "But I don't get mad about offers. What're you payin', Mister Fowler, for the first herd up this year?"

"Eighty dollar a head, payment on gate count into my corrals north of Wichita, Mister Howard."

Jess and Charles Spires exchanged a look. Spires's expression was like wood, but his eyes faintly gleamed. He took back a long drag off his cigar and blew it skyward. Jess lifted his rein hand. "See you again, Mister Fowler," he said, and turned his horse. "Potter, better make sure Gabe heads 'em far enough west."

"Wait!" Fowler called sharply. "The market's not established yet, Mister Howard. Yours is the first drive up the trail. I das'n't pay too much or I'll get bad hurt on the sellin' end in Chicago. And there's the shrink, y' know, three percent shrink on a thousand head between here an' Chicago in the cattle cars. . . ."

Jess regarded the older, shorter, and thicker man with a calm look. "Last summer late herds were fetchin' a hundred a head," he stated. "Maybe I'll just hang an' rattle a few days. There's no other herds close behind. I can afford to wait."

221

Fowler pinched his eyes nearly closed and turned for another long, long look at the closest animals. "Maybe we could ride through 'em," he suggested. "Down toward that wagon perhaps."

Jess shrugged and started off. Fowler and Spires poked along behind him. From time to time they'd bend close and utter a few words. When they were close to the wagon where Jonathan was hunched upon his seat, Fowler said: "Mister Howard, ninety dollars."

Jess rode on without turning his head.

Gabe and Potter swung the lead; all the other animals dutifully veered off away from the distant town, low and bulky upon the curving far horizon.

"Mister Howard. Confound it all, man, I'm takin' one hell of a chance."

That time Jess halted and turned his head. "Yeah," he murmured at Fowler. "You sure are."

"Well, then . . . one hundred dollars a head, and Charley'll cut back sick critters at the corrals."

"Mister Fowler," said Jess, "one hundred and ten a head . . . you take every damned one. Or . . . you take none at all."

"My God," squawked the cattle buyer, and rolled his eyes. "That's highway robbery, Mister Howard."

"Then," said Jess, "forget it." He lifted an arm to point. "More riders coming. More buyers, Mister Fowler. One hundred and ten a head, you take all . . . and bring out your own crew to take over tonight so I can pay off my men and get shed of the herd."

Abner Fowler looked daggers at Jess from between pinched-down lids. Charles Spires knocked ash from his smoke and softly grinned to himself. Jess kept watching the other horsemen while he waited for Fowler to wrestle with himself. He was lifting his reins to turn and lope over where those other men were approaching, when Fowler said: "All right, Mister Howard, it's done." He pushed out a massive paw to shake Jess's hand, which sealed the bargain. Jess shook, dropped Fowler's hand, and waited for the buyer to reach inside his coat for his draft book. As Ab Fowler grimly began writing, Jess and Charley Spires exchanged a surreptitious, dry wink.

Spires said: "I'll lope up to the point and have your men hold them, Jess. This is about as far west as I want the herd. Then I'll head on back for my crew. All right?"

Jess nodded. Spires wheeled and struck out for the yonder point riders. Ab Fowler finished drawing up the draft, ripped it out, and handed it over, along with a bill of sale for Jess to sign transferring title to Fowler. Jess signed, pocketed the draft, and heaved a mighty sigh. Those oncoming men were getting closer. Fowler pocketed his bill of sale and turned his horse. "I'll buy you a drink in town," he said. "See you then." As he loped away, he tipped his hat at the approaching horsemen, then sped on past them, outward bound.

The newcomers were not cattle buyers. One of

them had a badge on his shirt front. The others were armed with six-guns and carbines. When they halted, the lawman looked Jess up and down before he said: "You the trail boss?" Jess nodded. The lawman then said: "Did you have a little run-in with rustlers a few miles back?" Again Jess nodded. This time he made a closer inspection of the other riders, seeking a particular face. It wasn't there. If Jack Pruett had tried to make trouble, after all, he'd afterward lacked the courage to join the posse.

"Lose any men?" asked the peace officer.

"No."

The lawman gazed around and back again. "Pretty big herd to be movin' with no more men than you have," he said.

Jess's gaze hardened but he withheld comment. Potter and Gabe were loping down toward him from up where Charley Spires was blocking the herd, making it spread out, and slow to a grazing walk. Jonathan stopped his wagon, stood up on his seat to see why the herd wasn't going on, and off from the west Harper Ellis was making the big swing down around the drag also to ride over where he could see Jess and the others sitting their saddles. The lawman and his companions, five in number, watched all this. The lawman said: "My name's Clinton. Deputy Clinton from Wichita. I got at telegram about a feller named Levitt bein' with this Texas drive. Any truth in it?"

"He was with us," stated Jess. "If you heard that

224

much, then you also heard what happened down Prineville way."

The deputy, watching Potter and Gabe approach, nodded his head. "Yeah, I got that information, too." He kept eyeing saber-scarred, dark, and swarthy Potter Houston. "You happen to have any more wanted Texans with you, Mister Howard?"

"No," affirmed Jess. "And when I hired Wayne Levitt on, I didn't know he was wanted."

Gabe slowed and walked his horse around over behind Jess. He and Potter saw that badge and that unfriendly face over it. They halted and sat there stonily regarding the Kansas lawman.

"Any more questions?" asked Jess.

"Just one," said the lawman, turning to see Harper Ellis also approaching at a lope. "You had a lot of guts to make the first drive of the year with only six men. They tell me the renegades down Texas way are bad this spring. Is that right?"

"I had another rider. He was killed in a stampede. There were originally seven of us, all counted," answered Jess. "As for the renegades . . . yeah, they're bad this year."

The deputy nodded, his bleak gaze taking in Harper as the last Texan drifted up and stopped. He was obviously one of those cow-town deputies who could recognize outlaws on sight. As he lifted his rein hand, he said: "Sometime I wonder why you Texas boys do this for a livin'."

Jess had his answer ready. "I wouldn't swap my

job for yours, Deputy. The only thing I got to watch out for are rustlers, Comancheros, flash floods, stampedes, dry camps, and low prices."

The deputy made a small, tough smile at that, and inclined his head. "You might be right at that," he said. "Well, have a good time in town. Just keep any trigger-happy gents you got with you away from too big a load of Barleycorn. Otherwise, you boys bein' the first Texans up the trace this year, Wichita's yours to buck the tiger in an' to bay at the moon in. See you in town."

As the deputy and his companions rode off, Gabe said: "What was all that about?"

Jess shrugged. "A Kansas welcomin' committee," he stated. "He knew we had the brush with those sooners. I was waitin' for him to say something about it, but he never did."

"He knows," said Potter. "His kind always knows . . . we don't keep prisoners and we quietly bury the dead ones. Why should he squawk? It makes his job easier, don't it?"

They turned and drifted on down to the wagon where Jonathan was bustling around, setting up their final camp. He was croaking out a song called "The Cowboy's Lament", only he didn't know very many verses and had to improvise without any benefit of rhyme or reason.

The herd spread out; it seemed to perceive dimly, in the mysterious way dumb critters often do, that this was the end of the trail. Charley Spires, if he was still up there at the lead spot, wouldn't have much to do until Ab Fowler sent out the rest of his hired riders to take over and corral the herd well north of town where the shipping pens stood beside the railroad tracks. From now on, those Texas long-horns were someone else's responsibility.

Jess dug out his little leather bag, pushed back his hat, and went to work separating the coins into individual little stacks upon the camp wagon's scarred tailgate. What he had left over—Jeb's share and Wayne Levitt's share—he put into a different stack. Gabe and Harper and Potter were slicking up. They greased their boots, slicked down their hair. They even shaved and beat the dust out of their hats and trousers before putting on their clean, spare shirts. Wichita was theirs for one tumultuous night. Jonathan had camp set up in record time so that, when Jess called them around to the tailgate to be paid off, he was right there with his grimy paw stuck out along with the others.

Jess handed them their gold pieces. He nodded toward the remaining pile. "For Jeb's folks," he said. "Wayne wouldn't mind. Anyway, as far as I know, he left no kin behind."

Potter hefted his coins a moment, then collected several and lay them with the other little pile on the tailgate. Without a word Harper and Gabe stepped up also to contribute. Jonathan did the same. It made a sizeable little pile of gold coins. Jess dug into a pocket to do the same. He said: "I hope the folks who eat this beef never know what it cost to get it to them. They'd choke on it."

"Naw," muttered Jonathan, grimacing. "Not Yankees. They'd just eat all the more."

Potter turned his head. "Now what in hell have you got against Yankees?" he asked Jonathan, and the look of astonishment upon old Jonathan's face at such a remark from Yankee-hating Potter Houston made Gabe and Harper and Jess roar with laughter.

Jonathan sputtered. "You . . . why, dang it all, Potter Houston, I've stood an' heard you cuss out Yankees till the cows come home."

Potter didn't bat an eye. "Well, but that was *before*," he stoutly said.

"Before what, confound it all?" demanded Jonathan.

"Just you never mind," retorted the saber-scarred big Texan. "And furthermore you 'n' I're goin' into town together. There'll be no more of that business of you gettin' smoked to the gills and fallin' down on some saloon floor, fightin' a whole passel of renegades, makin' a fool of yourself."

Jonathan thought that over a moment before nodding and smiling. "Then let's go," he said. "Jess, we all paid off 'n' all?"

"You're free as birds. But I'm headin' back in the morning, so if you want half pay for tooling the camp wagon back, you'd better be able to drive and hitch up come daylight, Jonathan."

Potter gravely inclined his head. "He'll be able. I promise that. I'll go back with the pair of you."

"Me, too," said Gabe. "I got to make two more drives this year before I can spend next winter loafin'."

They all turned to gaze at Harper Ellis. He shook his head at them. "I told you what I'm going to do. Buy me a comfortable rockin' chair, drag it out here every spring, and watch you fellers grow old pushing those devil-tempered, ornery longhorns up the trail. Maybe get hitched and live in a house for a spell."

They started around to the texas where their saddled animals stood, heads hung, half asleep. They had covered all that bloody and lethal distance between Texas and the Kansas plains, had seen more men buried through violence than they'd originally numbered themselves, although only two of those dead men had been their friends, and now they had, by way of reward, one wild, tumultuous night ahead of them in Wichita, then back again to Texas, all but one of them, to do it all over again.

Potter wouldn't be going up the trail again. That left Jess and Gabe and Jonathan. The mortality rate was very high, fifty percent and better, but as Jess had once said, when he and Potter had talked of it, the Longhorn Trail had a way of drawing men to it, and forever after changing them.

About the Author

Lauran Paine who, under his own name and various pseudonyms has written over a thousand books, was born in Duluth, Minnesota. His family moved to California when he was at a young age and his apprenticeship as a Western writer came about through the years he spent in the livestock trade, rodeos, and even motion pictures where he served as an extra because of his expert horsemanship in several films starring movie cowboy Johnny Mack Brown. In the late 1930s, Paine trapped wild horses in northern Arizona and even, for a time, worked as a professional farrier. Paine came to know the Old West through the eyes of many who had been born in the previous century, and he learned that Western life had been very different from the way it was portrayed on the screen. "I knew men who had killed other men," he later recalled. "But they were the exceptions. Prior to and during the Depression, people were just too busy eking out an existence to indulge in Saturday-night brawls." He served in the U.S. Navy in the Second World War and began writing for Western pulp magazines following his discharge. It is interesting to note that all of his earliest novels (written under his own name and the pseudonym Mark Carrel) were published in the British market and he soon had as strong a following in that country as in the United States. Paine's Western fiction is characterized by strong plots, authenticity, an apparently effortless ability to construct situation and character, and a preference for building his stories upon a solid foundation of historical fact. *Adobe Empire* (1956), one of his best novels, is a fictionalized account of the last twenty years in the life of trader William Bent and, in an off-trail way, has a melancholy, bittersweet texture that is not easily forgotten. In later novels like *The White Bird* (1997) and *Cache Cañon* (1998), he showed that the special magic and power of his stories and characters had only matured along with his basic themes of changing times, changing attitudes, learning from experience, respecting Nature, and the yearning for a simpler, more moderate way of life.

Center Point Publishing
600 Brooks Road ● PO Box 1
Thorndike ME 04986-0001 USA

(207) 568-3717

US & Canada:
1 800 929-9108
www.centerpointlargeprint.com

Roblo.